"I'm just looking for tonight, Tom, not tomorrow or the day after...

"I want you and I can tell that you want me, too."

His breath caught in his throat as she moved to stand in front of him, so close he could feel her warm breath on his neck, so close her breasts touched his chest.

"We're not foolish kids, Tom. We're both adults and I can't think of a single reason why we can't make love tonight."

Frantically Tom tried to think of all the reasons it would be a bad idea, but he couldn't think at all as she wound her arms around his neck and pressed herself intimately against him.

"I'm not the man you want," he finally managed to say.

"You're the man I want right now," she replied. "And that's enough for me."

Dear Reader,

Most parents have had the misfortune of having a child
disappear for several horrifying moments. You look away
for a second and when you look back he or she is gone.

Once, when my daughter was three, we were out in the
front yard when the phone rang. I ran in to grab it and when
I came back outside a minute later she was gone. I found
her in a neighbor's yard, but I'll never forget the terror that
filled me in those first moments of not knowing where she
might have disappeared to.

When Peyton Wilkerson leaves her daughter in an infant
seat at the table and goes to retrieve something for her
friend, she's struck from behind. When she regains
consciousness she discovers that the friend and her baby girl
have vanished.

It takes the investigation of a committed sheriff and
Peyton's unwavering faith to get through the ordeal.
I hope you enjoy reading their story!

Thanks, and keep reading!

Carla Cassidy

CARLA CASSIDY

His Case, Her Baby

Silhouette®

Romantic

SUSPENSE

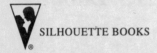

SILHOUETTE BOOKS

ISBN-13: 978-0-373-27670-7

HIS CASE, HER BABY

Copyright © 2010 by Carla Bracale

Printed in U.S.A.

Books by Carla Cassidy

Silhouette Romantic Suspense

CARLA CASSIDY

is an award-winning author who has written more than fifty books for Silhouette. In 1995, she won Best Silhouette Romance from *RT Book Reviews* for *Anything for Danny*. In 1998, she won a Career Achievement Award for Best Innovative Series.

Carla believes the only thing better than curling up with a good book to read is sitting down at the computer with a good story to write. She's looking forward to writing many more books and bringing hours of pleasure to readers.

Chapter 1

Peyton Wilkerson finished mopping her kitchen floor, pleased by the shine on the tiles and the clean scent of bleach that hung in the air. She put the mop away and then went to the window of the cozy ranch house.

She stared outside, where the day before the concrete company had poured a beautiful new patio inside the six-foot privacy fence that surrounded the backyard.

Pride ballooned in her chest. It was all finally coming together for her. After years of working two and three jobs, of attending college nights and weekends, some of her dreams were beginning to come true.

She not only had her very own house, but she also had a brand-new patio where she could have a barbecue and invite neighbors who would hopefully soon be friends.

She turned from the window at the sound of a soft coo coming from the portable infant rocking seat in the center of the kitchen table. Her heart swelled as she smiled at her four-month-old little girl.

"Hey, Lilly girl," Peyton said as she scooped the baby up in her arms. Lilly flailed her arms and cooed again, her rosebud little lips turning upward in a happy smile.

It almost frightened Peyton, how happy she'd become, how many of her dreams were beginning to blossom into fruition. In a month she would begin teaching first grade at the Black Rock Elementary School. And even though Lilly hadn't been planned, she was the greatest gift Peyton had ever been given.

Although things hadn't worked out between Peyton and Lilly's father, Rick, Rick had promised to be there for his daughter, and Peyton knew he'd do just that. He was a good man, just not the man for Peyton.

"Are you hungry?" Peyton asked as she placed Lilly back in her seat.

Lilly bounced and wiggled and smiled, a faint trail of drool making its way from her mouth to her chin. Peyton laughed and grabbed a towel to wipe her mouth. "Or would you rather I just get your piggies?" She grabbed Lilly's foot and tickled her toes. Lilly squealed and kicked her feet as Peyton laughed again.

The ringing of the doorbell interrupted the game. Making certain that Lilly was secure in the seat, Peyton left her and hurried to the door.

She peeked through the spy hole on the door and

saw the tall redhead on the other side. She quickly unfastened the dead bolt and opened the door. "Kathy! I didn't expect you to stop by today," she said.

"I decided a little exercise would do me good, so I thought I'd walk over for a visit, but it's hot as blazes out there." She flipped her long red hair over her shoulder and smiled. "Hope you don't mind a hot and thirsty friend dropping by unexpectedly."

"Not at all. Come on into the kitchen. I was just about to make a bottle for Lilly, and I'll get you something cold to drink."

As they entered the kitchen, Kathy beelined to Lilly as Peyton got a bottle of soda out of the fridge and set it on the table.

Kathy baby-talked to Lilly for a moment, then sat at the table and watched as Peyton prepared Lilly's bottle.

The two women had met two months earlier, right after Peyton had moved to the small western Kansas town. Kathy was new to town as well and the two had hit it off immediately.

"I see you got the patio poured," Kathy said as Peyton sat in the chair next to her and began to feed Lilly.

"Yesterday. I can't wait to have a real barbecue outside. I want to get one of those umbrella tables and invite all my new friends for burgers and hot dogs."

"At least wait until it cools down. This heat is about to kill me," Kathy exclaimed. "I'd forgotten how hot it gets in Kansas in July. Besides, you have to meet some new friends in order to invite them."

"I know, and I will," Peyton replied. "Now that I'm finally settled in and Lilly is getting older, I plan on getting out more." Peyton had been reluctant to take Lilly outside and around strangers while she'd been so small, and she'd had the work of settling in to keep her from going out and socializing.

"Did Rick stop by last night? You mentioned that he was planning on driving out to visit with the baby."

"No, he didn't make it. He's working some big trial and scarcely has time to breathe right now." Rick Powell was an assistant D.A. Handsome and ambitious, he and Peyton had dated for six months, and ironically Lilly had been conceived on the night they mutually decided to break up.

"He could have married you," Kathy said with a touch of censure.

Peyton laughed. "I didn't want to marry him. We had a great time together, but I realized I wasn't in love with him. Besides, Rick is already married to his work."

Lilly finished her bottle and yawned around the nipple. Almost immediately she closed her eyes and fell asleep. Peyton put her back in the cushioned seat in the center of the table and brushed a strand of the pale blond hair away from her forehead.

"She's such a doll baby," Kathy said, then frowned and raised a hand to her temple. "You don't happen to have anything for a headache, do you?"

"Nothing stronger than an aspirin," Peyton replied.

"Could I have a couple? I have a killer headache."

"Sure, hang on and I'll be right back. I've got a bottle under the sink in the bathroom."

"Great, thanks."

As Peyton walked through her living room with its gleaming polished surfaces and simple furnishings, she thought of how far she'd come from her roots.

She'd done it. She'd climbed out of the filth and the fear of her childhood. She was in a place where she couldn't get evicted, where filth would never exist again.

The guest bathroom in the hall was decorated in cool shades of mint-green and white. She straightened the hand towel next to the sink before she bent down to look for the aspirin bottle.

She was on her knees when she looked up and saw Kathy standing in the doorway. "Here you are," she said as she grabbed the bottle and began to rise.

"And here you are," Kathy said, and she slammed something into the side of Peyton's head. Peyton reeled backward, unable to keep her balance. *What? Why?* These two words exploded in Peyton's brain just before her head hit the edge of the bathtub and everything went black.

Consciousness came in bits and pieces. The faint scent of pine cleaner filled her nose and she winced from the nauseating pound of a headache. She opened her eyes and saw the mint-green bathroom rug beneath her face. She frowned in confusion. *What?* How did she get on the floor?

Kathy. Kathy had come into the bathroom and

attacked her. Kathy had hit her. As she got to her feet it all came back to her. Why? Why had her friend attacked her? It didn't make sense.

Lilly! She had to get to Lilly. The baby wasn't crying. Maybe she was still napping. Peyton's heart crashed against her ribs, like an off-balance washing machine on the spin cycle. Please, God, let her still be napping.

Woozy and unsteady on her feet, she stumbled down the hallway. She needed to call for help. She'd been attacked. But before she could do anything she needed her baby in her arms.

As she stepped into the kitchen she froze. The infant seat was in the center of the table, the receiving blanket a swath of rose color against the empty seat.

"No." The word whispered out of her as her knees buckled. Horror pressed against her chest, making it difficult for her to draw breath. Where was Lilly?

She reeled out of the kitchen and ran down the hall to Lilly's bedroom. Kathy must have put her in her crib. Even though Peyton knew it made no sense, that nothing made sense, she clung to the hope that Kathy had tucked Lilly into her crib before she'd left the house.

She clung to that tenuous, fragile hope as she raced into the small bedroom she'd decorated with pink ruffles and teddy bears. She stopped in the doorway and stared at the empty crib.

And screamed.

Sheriff Tom Grayson pulled his car into the driveway of the neat little ranch house and got out before the engine had completely shut off. His youngest brother, Caleb, waited for him on the lawn, his khaki deputy uniform the same color as the sunburned dried grass beneath his feet.

"What's up?" Tom asked. The late July heat felt as if it seared his lungs with each breath he took.

Caleb's brown eyes were darker than usual, a sure sign that he was troubled. "A missing baby."

Tom's stomach flipped. In all his years as sheriff of Black Rock, Kansas, there had never been a child missing or murdered.

"Details," Tom demanded.

"The woman, Peyton Wilkerson, says she was entertaining a friend and she went to the bathroom. She says the woman attacked her and knocked her unconscious, then stole the baby. But, I got to tell you, Tom, it all seems pretty fishy. Her wounds look superficial, she just had a new patio poured yesterday, and the kitchen smells like bleach."

Bleach, the best thing to use to clean up traces of blood. Tom tried to keep his mind open as he nodded and went into the house.

He stepped into the living room, and his first impression was one of obsessive neatness and order. The furnishings were simple and the room smelled of lemon furniture polish and glass cleaner.

He heard the sound of his brother Benjamin coming from the kitchen. It didn't surprise him that Benjamin was the one in the kitchen with the potential victim while Caleb had been the one pacing the grass outside.

Benjamin had an affinity for anyone he thought might be a victim of a crime. Softhearted to a fault, he would be consoling Peyton Wilkerson. On the other hand, impulsive, impatient Caleb was always ready to believe the worst in a situation, always ready to investigate and arrest.

Before going to the kitchen, Tom turned down a hallway and stepped into the first bedroom he came to. It was obviously a nursery. Decorated in shades of pink, it was tidy and held the faintest scent of baby lotion.

He left that room and went farther down the hall, passing a bedroom and coming to the master bedroom. Decorated in yellow, white and green, it gave the aura of a peaceful garden with sunshine. As with all the other rooms, nothing appeared out of place. Even the nightstand held nothing more than an attractive reading lamp.

Tom frowned as he thought of his own nightstand, which often held the remainder of a bedtime snack, whatever book he was currently reading and little notes to himself of things he thought of just before drifting off to sleep.

He touched nothing; he was just trying to get a quick feel for the person who lived there. So far he learned that Peyton Wilkerson definitely took pride in her surroundings and probably had more than a touch of obsessive-compulsiveness.

The first thing Tom noticed as he stood in the doorway to the kitchen was the faint, underlying scent of bleach. The second thing he noticed was that Peyton

Wilkerson was a stunner. Even red-rimmed eyes from crying and an angry gash on the side of her forehead couldn't detract from her fragile beauty.

Both she and Benjamin sat at the kitchen table. In the center of the table was an empty infant seat covered in pink material and ruffles.

Tom knew most of the people in the small town of Black Rock, but he'd never seen Peyton Wilkerson before. If he had, he definitely would have remembered.

As he stepped into the room she jumped up from her chair. "Thank God," she said, tears shimmering in her already swollen eyes as she reached out and grabbed his hand. "Sheriff, you have to do something. You have to go get my Lilly."

Her hand was fevered and trembled in his. The sense of urgency that he'd felt when Caleb had told him a baby was missing welled up inside him.

"Who took her?" Tom asked.

"Her name is Kathy Simon, and she lives in the Black Rock Apartments. Please, we have to get my baby back. She's only four months old." A sob escaped her as Tom led her back to the chair where she'd been seated.

"You know what apartment she lives in?" he asked, aware that Caleb had come into the room.

Peyton frowned. "No, not specifically. Whenever I've dropped her off, it's always been at the front entrance."

"What does she look like?" Tom asked.

"She has shoulder-length red hair and blue eyes.

She's taller than me and very thin. She told me she was twenty-nine, the same age as me."

"Caleb, Benjamin, head over to the apartments and check it out," Tom said. "Get out an AMBER Alert and have Sam run a check on a Kathy Simon. Tell Clay and Eric to set up roadblocks on both ends of town and to check every car leaving town."

"I want to go to the apartments, too," Peyton exclaimed.

"You and I are going to stay here so I can ask you some questions," Tom said firmly. "My deputies will check things out." He nodded in dismissal to his brothers, who immediately left.

He returned his attention to Peyton, who looked as if she were hanging onto her very sanity by a thread. "Tell me what happened this morning."

For a moment he thought she was going to break down altogether. Her lips trembled and tears filled her eyes. "Please, Mrs. Wilkerson. I know this is difficult, but the more information I have the easier it will be to find your baby."

She drew a deep breath and visibly pulled herself together. "I had just finished cleaning the kitchen when Kathy showed up." She gripped a tissue in her hand so tightly her knuckles were white.

"I smell bleach. Is that what you were cleaning with?" he asked.

She nodded. "I always use a little bleach when I clean, especially when I mop the floor."

Tom watched her carefully, trying to discern any

deceit in the depths of her blue eyes. "You and this Kathy, you were friends?"

She nodded, a single curt nod. The sunshine streaming through the window sparkled in her pale blond hair. "We met about two months ago, right after I moved here. She was new to Black Rock, too, and we hit it off right away."

Tom pulled a small notepad and a pen from his pocket.

"You have a phone number for her?"

"No, she told me she didn't have a phone. She said she was short on money and had to cancel her cell phone and hadn't yet gotten a landline."

"What about a car? Do you know what kind she drove?"

She raised a trembling hand to her forehead and frowned. "I don't know. She mentioned something about it being in the shop."

"Do you know where she was from?"

Her frown deepened, the gesture doing nothing to detract from her attractiveness. "Chicago, I think."

"Where's your husband? Can I call him for you?"

She shook her head. "I'm not married. Lilly's father lives in Wichita."

"What's his name?" Tom asked. Maybe this was some sort of parental kidnapping, he thought. God, he hoped so. At least then he'd know the baby was safe.

"Rick, Rick Powell," she replied. Her eyes widened. "Surely you don't think he had anything to do with this.

He wouldn't. He's an assistant district attorney. He'd never be part of anything like this," she exclaimed.

She scooted back from the table and jumped up, her slender body vibrating with energy. "We don't have time to sit here and talk. I need to find Lilly." She reached up and grabbed the back of her head and grimaced.

Tom wouldn't have thought her face could get any paler, but it blanched of any lingering color. He jumped to his feet and grabbed her by the arm. "Are you all right? Do you need medical attention?"

She dropped her hand to her side, her body weaving slightly. "I sent the ambulance away. I'm all right. I just hit my head on the bathtub when she attacked me."

She allowed Tom to guide her back into the chair at the table. He could smell her, a scent of fresh flowers and despair, and he tried to maintain emotional distance, knowing that it was possible that all was not what it seemed.

As he asked her about the particulars of the attack and listened to her answers, he assessed the kitchen which was now a crime scene.

Did she like things so neat and clean, or had she sanitized the house before calling for help? Had a terrible accident taken place here and now she was trying to cover it up?

Certainly the news was full of stories of babies who had been shaken to death or suffocated by an overwrought parent. Or was it as she said, and a kidnapping had really occurred? It was too early to know the truth.

As quickly as possible, Tom got the pertinent information from her, and then he called in two of his deputies to fingerprint and collect evidence from the bathroom and the kitchen. He called another deputy to check with the garage to see if Kathy Simon had a car being worked on there.

With the arrival of the two deputies, Tom moved Peyton into the living room, where she paced the floor and looked as if she were about ready to jump out of her skin.

Tom had placed a call to Rick Powell and had gotten in touch with his secretary, as Rick was in trial. She'd promised to pass a message to him as soon as possible for him to call Tom.

Peyton had been seated on the sofa, hands wringing and her delicate features taut with tension as Tom directed his deputies attempting to lift fingerprints from the surfaces Kathy might have touched.

Although she appeared calm, but stressed, Tom sensed an explosion coming. He saw it in the white of her knuckles as she folded her hands together, in the deepening hue of her blue eyes as she watched him.

So far she'd been patient and cooperative, but he had a feeling that that was coming to an end quickly. As if to prove his intuition, she sprang up from the sofa when the phone rang.

The tight composure she'd kept cracked as she tearfully told Rick what had happened. Rick promised to come as soon as possible, but it was a two-and-a-half-hour drive from Wichita to Black Rock.

"You have to do something," she exclaimed after she'd hung up with Rick. For the first time there was an edge of frantic anger in her voice. "Why haven't we heard something? What's taking so long?"

Tom had been thinking the same thing. "We should hear something from them any minute. We have the AMBER Alert out and I have a deputy checking background on Kathy. At this point there's nothing else we can do but wait here until we have more information." He glanced toward her phone.

She followed his gaze, then looked back at him, her eyes widening slightly. "You think maybe she'll call?" A half-hysterical sob escaped her. "She won't call. This isn't about a ransom. Kathy knows I don't have any money."

"Then what do you think this is about?"

"I don't know," she cried. "I feel like this is all some horrible joke, or a terrible nightmare. I can't imagine why Kathy did this. I just can't wrap my mind around all of this."

She whirled around as the door opened and Caleb and Benjamin walked in. Caleb gave a small shake of his head.

"What does that mean?" Peyton asked. "Why are you shaking your head?"

"There's no Kathy Simon living at the Black Rock Apartments," he said.

"What do you mean? I know she lives there. I dropped her off there several times." Peyton looked from Caleb to Tom, then back to Caleb again.

"We checked with the manager. There's no Kathy Simon on a lease. We also knocked on every door and asked if anyone knew her. Nobody did," Benjamin added.

Peyton's eyes widened in horror as she looked at Tom. "Then where is she? And where has she taken my Lilly?"

Chapter 2

Peyton felt as if the ground beneath her feet was no longer solid. The world was no longer as it should be, and she'd never felt such fear. *Lilly!* Her heart cried in anguish. Where was her baby?

Who was Kathy Simon, and why had she done this? Had anything she'd told Peyton about herself been true? One thing was certain: Peyton had wasted enough time sitting around waiting for something to happen.

She needed to find Lilly, and she wasn't going to find her sitting around and answering questions. Without saying a word to the sheriff or his deputies, she headed down the hall to her bedroom.

Sheriff Grayson followed just behind her, as if afraid to let her out of his sight for a minute. "What are you doing?" he asked as she grabbed her purse from the top of her dresser.

"I'm going to find my baby." She turned to face him. "If I have to knock on every door of this town, I'll find Kathy and my Lilly."

"I don't think that's a good idea," he protested.

She raised her chin and embraced the anger that was so much easier to tolerate than her pain. "The only way you're going to stop me, Sheriff Grayson, is to arrest me and lock me up."

Despite the fact that he was easily six inches taller than her and had shoulders as broad as mountains, she shoved roughly past him and headed for the front door.

She'd gone only a couple of steps when he grabbed her by the arm. "I'll take you wherever you want to go." His dark eyes held her gaze intently. "We don't know if this woman is dangerous. She might not harm your baby, but she would definitely be a threat to you."

She considered his words and gave him a curt nod. "Then let's go. I can't sit here another minute."

She was vaguely surprised to see that the sun was still high in the sky. It had been less than two hours since Kathy and Lilly had disappeared, but it felt like an eternity.

Even the intensity of the late afternoon sun overhead couldn't warm the glacier that had become Peyton's heart. She slid into the passenger seat of the sheriff's car and was instantly engulfed by the scent of leather and, more faintly, the spicy cologne he wore.

As he got in behind the steering wheel he turned to look at her. "Do you have a plan?"

She'd shot out of the house lit with the fire of a frantic mother seeking her child, but she realized with the question that she didn't have a plan; she just knew she couldn't sit still another minute.

"The pizza place on Main Street," she said suddenly. "Kathy told me she was working there until she could get something more permanent."

He nodded, started the car and pulled away from the curb. Peyton stared out the window, irrationally hoping that Kathy would suddenly appear on the sidewalk.

The only thing that kept Peyton from losing her mind altogether was the belief that Kathy wouldn't hurt Lilly. "She was good with Lilly," she finally said aloud. "She seemed to love her."

"Did you mention wanting children of her own, maybe not being able to have them?" Sheriff Grayson asked.

"No, nothing like that. I just know she was always very sweet to Lilly. Surely the pizza place will have her address on file."

"What I need you to do is think of all the conversations you had with her, any tidbit of information that might be helpful as to where she might go and who she might be with," he replied.

For a moment Peyton was overwhelmed. "Sheriff Grayson, we talked almost every day, about everything and nothing." She frowned and tried to ignore the headache that pounded in the back of her head, the continuous frantic race of her heart.

"Call me Tom," he said. "There are four of us Graysons working law enforcement in Black Rock. First names make things easier."

"Caleb and Benjamin are your brothers?" she asked.

He nodded. "My sister is also a deputy, then I have one other brother who doesn't work for the town of Black Rock." He frowned. "Did Kathy mention dating somebody here in town? Perhaps somebody she was interested in?"

"No, in fact just the opposite. I got the impression she was a bit shy and was having trouble meeting people." She released a sigh of frustration. "God, what did I miss? What didn't I see or hear in all those conversations, in all the time we spent together?"

"You can't beat yourself up about that. How could you guess that something like this would happen?" He pulled into a parking space in front of the Canyon Pizzeria and cut the engine, then he turned and looked at her with his dark, intense eyes. "You let me ask the questions. I need to do my job."

She nodded and unbuckled her seatbelt, butterflies like little kamikaze pilots hitting the sides of her stomach. *Please, let us get some answers,* she thought as she got out of the car.

It was nearing dinnertime and the air outside the restaurant smelled of tangy tomato sauce and baking crust. The food smells only upset Peyton's stomach even more. The last thing she was interested in was food.

All she wanted was her sweet Lilly back in her arms.

She needed to smell her baby scent, feel Lilly's wiggly warmth against her chest.

She followed Sheriff Grayson through the front door. Inside, about a dozen people were seated at various tables and booths. Most of them raised a hand in greeting to the sheriff.

He went to the woman standing behind the cash register. "Hey, Linda, is Don in?" he asked.

"He's in the back. You here to arrest him for spicy sauce?" The blonde gave him a saucy, flirtatious smile.

"I need to talk to him. Can you get him out here?"

Her smile faded as she apparently heard the seriousness in his voice. "Sure, I'll go get him."

She disappeared into the kitchen and a moment later a big burly man clad in a tomato-splattered apron walked out.

"Hey, Tom. What's up?"

"You have a Kathy Simon working here for you?" Tom asked.

Peyton watched in horror as Don shook his head. "I've got a Stacy, a Katie and a Linda, but no Kathy," he replied.

"Are you sure? Maybe she was going by another name," Peyton said desperately. "She's tall with red hair?"

"Sorry, nobody like that works for me," Don replied.

Peyton staggered back outside where dusk was beginning to fall, vaguely aware of the sheriff right behind her. Nothing Kathy had told her had been true. She'd lied about where she worked, where she lived. Why?

She got back into the passenger seat and Tom slid in behind the wheel. "You okay?" he asked as he started the engine.

"Of course I'm not okay." She reached for anger, knowing that if she didn't hang on to something she'd lose it altogether. "Nothing she told me was the truth. Why would she lie to me about the most basic things? God, she was good. She had so many details. She told me about a man who had tipped her twenty dollars, about a little girl who wanted pizza crust and cheese but no sauce. She was so good with her lies."

A sickness welled up inside her as she realized night was falling too quickly and she was no closer to finding Lilly than she'd been when she'd regained consciousness on her bathroom floor.

"Any other ideas?" Tom asked as he backed out of the parking space in front of the pizza place. "Or are you ready to go back to your place?"

"No, we can't go back," she exclaimed. She didn't want to be there without her baby. "Just drive around. Maybe we'll see something."

For the next thirty minutes he drove up and down the streets of the small town. Peyton kept her gaze on the sidewalks, on the houses they passed, hoping for a glimpse of the woman she knew as Kathy Simon.

He received only one phone call during the drive.

When he hung up he told her that there was no driver's license matching what they knew about Kathy Simon.

"So that's probably not her real name," Peyton said flatly. She was numb; in a place where her fear was so great she couldn't process it any longer.

"Probably not," he agreed.

"How are we going to find her if we don't even know her name?" Peyton wanted to scream.

"We'll figure it all out," he replied. "Have you had any problems with anyone here in town?"

"No, nobody. Oh, there was a young man who cussed me in the parking lot of the grocery store. I was getting Lilly into her car seat and my shopping cart accidentally rolled into his truck."

"Did you exchange information?"

"No, nothing like that. It didn't scratch or dent the truck. He cursed me, then got in his truck and roared off."

"When did this happen?"

"About a week ago. Surely you don't think that has anything to do with Lilly's kidnapping," she said.

"I'm not taking anything for granted at this point," he replied. "What did this guy look like? What kind of a truck was he driving?"

"It was a black pickup, but I don't know the year or model. He was tall with brown hair." She sighed in frustration. "That doesn't help much, does it?"

"Sounds like half the men around this area," he replied.

As he once again drove down Main Street, Peyton

knew this probably wasn't standard operating procedure, that he was just indulging her need to be out looking. She also knew that there was no way she would see Kathy casually walking down the street with Lilly in her arms. She knew in her heart that Kathy had probably run out of town mere minutes after grabbing Lilly.

"I noticed you had a new patio in your backyard."

Peyton shifted her gaze from the window to him. "It was poured yesterday. What does that have to do with anything?"

"Just curious."

She stared at him, her heart beating an unsteady rhythm. She had a feeling this man didn't indulge in idle curiosity. There was a sharp intelligence in his sexy dark eyes that made her believe he was a man who didn't miss much.

As the realization of what he might be thinking struck her, she gasped. "You can't really believe that I had the patio poured to hide my baby's body?"

"It doesn't matter what I believe. I have to think of all possible scenarios," he said without apology.

"Pull over," she exclaimed. "I think I'm going to be sick."

He whirled the car to the curb and she unbuckled her seat belt, opened the door and stumbled outside. She bent over, feeling the need to throw up. He thought she'd killed her baby. He thought she'd killed her Lilly and buried her beneath the patio.

She dry heaved, her stomach rolling as tears blurred her vision. She was vaguely aware of a big, broad hand on her back, and she shook it off, the need to be sick swallowed by a rage she'd never felt before.

Her rage wasn't directed at Sheriff Tom Grayson, who was just doing his job, but rather at the woman who had pretended to be her friend and support over the past two months. The woman who had hit her in the head and stolen her baby.

She finally straightened up and stared at the sheriff. "If and when we find her, if she's hurt Lilly in any way, I'll kill her." She didn't wait for his reply but instead turned and walked back to the car and got into the passenger seat.

It was at that moment, with the fire of rage burning in her eyes, that Tom believed her. He hadn't been one hundred percent sure what to believe up until that point. There had been far too many cases of murdered children when the mothers concocted a story to cover the fact that they'd either accidentally or purposely hurt or killed their child.

He liked to believe he was good at assessing people, at recognizing liars and criminals. He didn't believe Peyton was either, and that meant they had a missing baby on their hands.

When they pulled up to her house, a luxury sports car was parked in the driveway. "That's Rick's car," she said, emotion thick in her voice.

As she and Tom got out of his car, the front door of the house opened and a tall, well-dressed blond man stepped out.

Peyton ran toward him, and Tom would have expected Rick to open up his arms, to hug the woman who was the mother of his missing child. But she stopped just short of him and Rick shoved his hands in his expensive slacks pockets. "What exactly happened?" he asked.

Peyton began to cry as she explained to him what had occurred. When she was finished, Rick looked at Tom. "Sheriff, Rick Powell." He held out his hand to Tom. "What's being done to find my daughter?"

Tom gave his hand a perfunctory shake, then motioned toward the front door. "Why don't we all go inside and talk."

As he followed them inside he found himself wishing that Rick had hugged her. If anyone needed the security of strong arms around her, it was Peyton. The thought hit him from left field and he pushed it aside.

"We have an AMBER Alert in place, and several of my deputies are out knocking on doors and seeing if anyone knows this woman who called herself Kathy Simon," Tom explained once they were all seated at the table. "It would be helpful if we could get a picture or a drawing of this woman to send out across the state."

"Do you have a picture of her?" Rick asked Peyton.

"No, I never took her picture," Peyton said miserably.

"My brother Benjamin is a pretty good artist. Why don't I get him in here to work up a sketch, and Rick and I can go into the living room and talk," Tom said.

Peyton nodded as he and Rick stood. Within minutes,

Benjamin was seated with her at the table, and Rick and Tom went into the living room, where Rick sat on the sofa and looked at Tom expectantly.

"Peyton told me you're an assistant D.A. in Wichita," Tom said.

"That's right." He leaned forward and ran a hand through his short hair. "I can't believe this has happened. Peyton's a terrific mother. She would never intentionally put Lilly at risk."

"You have no idea who this woman might be? You never met her?"

"No, but I have to confess that since Peyton moved here I've only been to visit a couple of times," Rick replied. "With my work schedule it's been difficult getting back and forth. In fact, I'm in the middle of a big trial now. I got the judge to call a continuance until day after tomorrow, but I've got to be back in Wichita first thing Thursday morning. Hopefully we'll have Lilly back long before then."

"Why did Peyton decide to move here?" Tom asked.

Rick leaned back in the chair and unfastened the buttons of his suit coat. "When our relationship fizzled out, she decided she wanted a new start someplace else. She started shooting out résumés, and when Black Rock Elementary School made an offer, she jumped at the opportunity."

"Your breakup was amicable?"

Rick released a small sigh of impatience. "Look, Sheriff, I know how these things go. I understand that you have to look at all angles, but let me save you a little time. Peyton and I dated for six months. We had a good time together but eventually realized we wanted different things from life. The split was amicable. In fact, it was the night we decided to call it quits that Lilly was conceived. Even though we weren't going to be together as a couple, we were both excited to be parents. We've had no problems, no issues since Lilly's birth. Peyton is one of the greatest women I've ever known. She would never do anything to hurt Lilly, and neither would I."

Tom fought back a sigh of frustration. He knew Rick was trying to be helpful, but there was nothing worse than investigating somebody who knew the system from the inside out. "You know I have to go through all this," Tom said.

Rick nodded. "I was just trying to cut to the chase by letting you know that there's nothing to investigate except the woman who stole my daughter. There's no point in wasting time speculating about Peyton or myself."

"I appreciate your help, but you know I'm going to do this investigation my way," Tom said. He kept his voice friendly but firm.

"Understood," Rick replied. "I just want my little girl back." For the first time since he'd arrived, emotion cracked his voice.

"Is it possible this has something to do with a case you're working on? An enemy you've made through your work?" Tom asked.

Rick frowned thoughtfully. "I don't think so. Very few people knew about Peyton and the baby. I wanted it that way for their own protection."

At that moment, Benjamin and Peyton came into the room. "We have a sketch," Benjamin said. He handed the paper to Tom, who looked at it closely.

Benjamin was a talented sketch artist, a talent he'd kept hidden for many years. The sketch showed a woman with a slender face and long hair. Her eyes were slightly deep set and her chin square.

Tom looked up at Peyton. "This looks like Kathy Simon?"

"It could be a photograph of her." For the first time her eyes shone with a hint of hope. Tom was struck again by her prettiness.

He handed the sketch to Rick. "Have you seen this woman?"

Rick studied the sketch with a frown, then shook his head. "No, I've never seen her before."

Tom looked back at Peyton. "You have a recent picture of Lilly?"

"I do. I just had her pictures taken at that little studio on Main Street a couple of weeks ago." She went to the desk in the corner of the room and opened a drawer. She withdrew a large envelope and from it pulled a 5x7 photograph.

She gazed at the picture for a long moment, her eyes filling with tears, then she handed it to Tom. Lilly was a doll, one of those exceptionally pretty babies with bright blue eyes and a tuft of curly blond hair.

Tom turned to his brother Caleb, who had returned to the house moments earlier after interviewing more of the people who lived in and around the apartment complex. "Take these to the office and get them over the wires," he said as he handed the photo and sketch to him. "Make up flyers and get them distributed around town."

When Caleb went out the front door, Tom turned back to Peyton. "Somebody will see them. Somebody will know where she is," he said in encouragement.

"I hope so," Peyton exclaimed.

The next couple of hours passed in agonizing slowness. Peyton sat on the sofa looking as if a loud noise might shatter her. Rick sat next to her, but at no time did the two touch in any way.

Tom found their relationship rather intriguing. Was their lack of physical touch an indication that their relationship hadn't had the mutual easy ending that both of them had implied? And what, if anything, might that have to do with the case?

Throughout the evening, Tom coordinated efforts to find the baby, speaking to his deputies by cell phone to keep updated. As night fell, Tom didn't expect anything to happen. People were in their homes, getting ready for bed, and wouldn't see the flyers until morning.

Rick must have recognized the same thing. At tenthirty he stood. "I checked into the hotel downtown when I arrived. I think I'll head over there for the rest of the night. I'm in room 112. Somebody will let me know if anything happens?"

"Of course," Tom replied, vaguely surprised by his decision to leave.

Rick reached down and grabbed Peyton's hand. "Stay strong," he said. "I'm sure we'll have her back tomorrow." He dropped her hand and with a nod to Tom left the house.

Almost immediately, Peyton got up from the sofa and went to the front window. She stared out with her back to Tom, and he was struck by how alone, how achingly fragile, she looked.

"Do you have children, Tom?" She didn't turn to face him but remained staring out the window into the darkness of the night.

"No wife, no kids," he replied. He stepped closer to her, close enough that he could smell the pleasant scent of her perfume.

"So you can't know what this feels like." She turned to face him and raw pain radiated from her eyes.

"No, I can't know exactly what it feels like," he said softly.

"I feel like Kathy reached inside my chest and ripped my heart out." Tears slid down her cheeks. "Nothing matters except Lilly. I need her back, Tom. I need her back in my arms." A deep sob exploded out of her and she nearly crumpled to the floor.

Before she could, Tom reached out for her and pulled her tight against his chest. She sagged against him and buried her face in the front of his shirt while she cried.

He wrapped his arms around her and held tight,

knowing it was the only comfort he could offer her at the moment. As he held her he went over it all in his mind, satisfying himself that everything that could be done was being done.

Now it became a waiting game. Hopefully somebody knew this woman who had called herself Kathy Simon, somebody who would call with information that would lead them to her and the baby.

But the last time Tom had held a weeping woman in his arms, everything had ended badly. Tragedy had pulled her away from him, and he'd nearly been destroyed.

He hoped at the end of all this that Peyton would have her baby safely back in her arms. He hadn't been strong enough to help one woman deal with grief, and he prayed he wouldn't have to help Peyton.

Chapter 3

Peyton didn't realize how much she'd needed to be held until Tom's strong arms surrounded her. The fact that it was a relative stranger's arms that brought her some comfort wasn't lost on her. But his arms were solid and warm and the clean, slightly spicy scent of him was comforting, making her reluctant to leave his embrace.

She finally raised her face to look up at him. "Thank you. I needed somebody to hold me for just a minute or two." Reluctantly she dropped her hands from around his neck and stepped back from him. "As you probably noticed, Rick isn't very good in the hug department."

"Yeah, I noticed that. Why don't you make some coffee for us?" he asked as he took her by the elbow and led her back into the kitchen. "You should probably try to eat something, too," he said as he leaned against the counter.

She shook her head. "I can't even think about food right now, but if you're hungry I have some sandwich stuff."

"Sure, I'd take a sandwich," he replied.

As the coffee began to fill the air with its fragrance and Peyton got out the lunch meat and cheese to build a sandwich, she realized he was keeping her busy, trying to keep her mind off the reason he was here, the reason Lilly wasn't in her bouncy chair on the table.

When she finished making the sandwich she set it on the table in front of Tom. She poured them each a cup of coffee and joined him there.

She still wanted to weep and wail, to walk the streets and rip open each and every door she came to in order to find Lilly, but she knew in all likelihood that Kathy was long gone. She also knew Tom had set in place the means that would hopefully find her baby.

"It's going to be a long night," she said aloud as her gaze drifted toward the window where the darkness was profound. "I can't believe she's out there somewhere and not here with me."

"Tell me about your relationship with Rick," he said.

She looked back at him and knew he was once again trying to take her mind off Lilly—as if that were possible. Still, she wanted conversation. She wanted to talk about everything and anything so that she wouldn't hear the screaming voice inside her head that said her baby was gone.

She wrapped her cold fingers around the warmth of her coffee cup and frowned. "There isn't a whole lot to tell. I met Rick in a coffee shop where I was working near the courthouse in Wichita. He was handsome and charming, and when he asked me out I was thrilled. We got close really fast, but it didn't take me long to realize I would never be first in Rick's life. I'd always be a distant third behind his work and his colleagues. For a while I was okay with that. But toward the end I realized that for once in my life I wanted to be the first priority in somebody's life, and it wasn't going to happen with Rick."

She paused and took a sip of her coffee. "Anyway, we both agreed that we weren't right for each other and had one last fling that resulted in Lilly."

"A surprise?"

"Definitely," she replied. "But, the minute I saw the test result and knew that I was pregnant, I also knew I wanted the baby more than I'd ever wanted anything in my life."

"And what about Rick? How did he feel about it?"

She frowned thoughtfully. "Initially I think he was a little bit upset. Any man would be. Neither of us had planned to become parents so soon, but he quickly came around. He was one hundred percent supportive through the pregnancy and was right there with me when Lilly was born."

"What about support and visitation rights? Did you

work those out legally?" His chocolate-brown eyes seemed to see everything that was inside her soul.

"No. I know Rick will do the right thing where Lilly is concerned, and if he doesn't then I'll be fine on my own." For the first time since this horror had begun, she noticed that Sheriff Tom Grayson was a very handsome man. The warmth of his dark brown eyes tempered the stern, stark lines of his face.

She leaned back in her chair, slightly disconcerted by her spark of feminine interest. "Anyway, I figured if Rick wants to be a part of Lilly's life he'll make that happen. I didn't want some legal form to bind him to us if he didn't want that."

"You said for once in your life you wanted to be somebody's priority. What about your parents?" He took a bite of his sandwich and looked at her expectantly.

"I never knew my father, and I was always a distant third in my mother's life, right behind her drugs and her newest boyfriend." She couldn't hide the touch of bitterness that crept into her voice.

"Doesn't sound like the makings of a great childhood," he said softly.

"It wasn't." She stared back out the window, tossed back into painful memories she tried never to access. "It was nothing but fear and uncertainty and one cheap, filthy motel room after another." She looked back at him. "I promised myself then that if I survived eventually I'd have a place of my own that would never be dirty, a place where nobody could kick me out onto the streets."

He took another bite of his sandwich and looked around. "Looks like you've succeeded."

She nodded. "It's taken a long time to get here, but I'm happy where I'm at," she replied. "But now that somebody has taken my Lilly—"

Emotion clawed up the back of her throat, and she felt as if the darkness outside the window were seeping into her blood, taking over her heart. Just as she thought she'd be swallowed whole, Tom reached across the table and grabbed her hand tight in his.

"We're doing everything that can be done to find them," he said. "You have to stay strong. You said you didn't think Kathy would hurt Lilly. You have to believe that, hang on to that."

She squeezed his hand and nodded. "I do believe that. She was good with Lilly." She released a sigh. "Maybe she can't have children of her own. Maybe she only befriended me because she wanted Lilly."

He released her hand and leaned back in his chair. "If that's the case, then somebody in her life will realize she suddenly has a baby. She can't stay underground forever. Somewhere somebody is going to see her and Lilly and make a phone call."

"You sound so optimistic," she said.

He smiled then. It was the first real smile she'd seen on his face, and it was a nice one. It softened the sternness and deepened the warmth of his eyes. "I'm generally an optimist. I'd rather think on the positive side unless I have a reason to think otherwise."

"What's positive about all this?" she asked, needing something, anything to hang on to.

"It's encouraging to me that she didn't kill you. According to you, you blacked out and you aren't sure how long you were out. She would have had a perfect opportunity to kill you then, but she didn't. I'd rather be chasing a kidnapper than a killer."

He got up from the table and walked over to the coffeemaker. For a big man he moved with an innate grace, as if perfectly comfortable in his own skin. He picked up the coffee carafe and carried it to the table.

"No more for me," she said. He filled his cup, then returned the pot to the machine and once again sat down across from her.

"Your brother doesn't believe my story about Kathy, about anything I said," she said. "He thinks I did something to Lilly." The very idea threatened to squeeze the breath from her lungs.

Once again a small smile raced across his features. "Caleb is the cynic in the family. Half the time he doesn't believe anything I tell him."

"Tell me about the rest of your family." She needed something to take her mind off the ticking of the clock, off the deepening of the night and the fact that her baby girl wasn't in her crib where she belonged.

"I'm the eldest. I'm thirty-six. Jacob is next. He's thirty-four. He's the only one of us who didn't hang around Black Rock. Instead of joining the sheriff's department like all of us did, he became an FBI agent, working out of the Kansas City field office. A little over a month ago he quit his job and came back to Black Rock. He's been staying in a little cottage we have on the ranch property." A deep frown furrowed his forehead and he glanced out the window as if in deep thought.

"You're worried about him," Peyton said softly.

His gaze shot back to her. "Yeah, I guess I am. He hasn't told any of us what brought him home. He refuses to leave the cottage and has become a recluse." He shrugged. "I guess he'll tell us what's going on when the time is right."

"And what about the others? Benjamin seemed very kind."

"Benjamin is the softie of the family. Even when he was a kid he was trying to save the whales, adopt a pet, sponsor a starving child or whatever to help. Besides being a terrific deputy he also runs the family ranch on the northern edge of town."

"And you mentioned a sister?"

This time his smile was full of fond indulgence. "Brittany, she's twenty-four and the baby of the family. She's also a deputy."

"What about your parents? You haven't mentioned them."

"They died six years ago in a private plane crash. They were adventure junkies. The minute we were all old enough to take care of ourselves, they disappeared to one exotic location or another. The end result was that it made us kids closer than most big broods. What about your mother? Where is she now?"

"She died in prison when I was eighteen. I was

thirteen when she was arrested for manufacturing meth. She went to prison and I went into the foster care system. Unfortunately, I wasn't one of their success stories, and when I turned sixteen I ran away."

She couldn't believe she was telling him all this. Usually she was reticent to share the details of her ugly past with anyone. She hadn't even told Rick much about her childhood.

Maybe it was because it was dark and the middle of the night and she was feeling especially vulnerable. Or perhaps it was because his eyes were soft and without judgment and there was a solidness about him that made her think she could tell him anything.

"Sounds like things haven't been easy for you," he said.

She shrugged. "They say what doesn't kill you makes you strong." The darkness that she'd tried to push away all night suddenly slammed into her. An unexpected sob caught in the back of her throat.

"If anything happens to Lilly, it won't make me strong," she exclaimed. "It will kill me, Tom. It will honestly kill me."

As she began to cry once again he stood and pulled her back into his arms. This time his embrace not only felt welcomed, but familiar. She leaned into him, absorbing the strength she instinctively knew he possessed.

If she could just get through this night, then surely Lilly would come home. All she had to do was get through the agonizing long, dark night.

* * *

It was four in the morning when Peyton finally fell into an exhausted sleep in a chair in the living room. Tom considered moving her to her bedroom but was afraid in rousing her she would never go back to sleep, and she needed to sleep.

So did he.

When he was sure she was down for the count, he called Benjamin to come and sit with her so Tom could head home for a couple hours of sleep.

As he waited for Benjamin to arrive, he thought of everything that had been done so far in an effort to find Kathy Simon and the missing baby. Throughout the evening there had been a steady influx of deputies checking in to tell him what had been accomplished.

The sketch and picture of Lilly had gone over the wire services, the AMBER Alert was in effect and everything that could be done was being done. Now it was just a matter of time.

He met Benjamin at the front door and motioned him into the kitchen. "Hopefully she'll sleep for a couple of hours."

Benjamin nodded. "And hopefully in the next couple of hours we'll start getting some phone calls that will lead us to the baby."

"I'm going to catch an hour or two of sleep then head into the office and coordinate things. I'll try to be back here by noon."

"You okay?" Benjamin asked, his brow furrowed with concern. "I know this one must be tough for you."

"No tougher than any other," Tom replied curtly. There was no way he'd admit to his brother that for just a moment, as he'd looked at the photograph of Lilly, he'd remembered another little girl and an unexpected knife had pierced through his heart.

He shoved this thought away as he left Peyton's house and got into his patrol car. A deep weariness gripped him as he drove the short drive home.

He hoped Peyton was right and this Kathy character wouldn't harm the baby, and he hoped that when morning dawned phone calls would start flooding into the office, tips from people who either knew or had seen the woman calling herself Kathy Simon.

Tom's house was a white two-story with a wrap-around porch and hunter green shutters at the windows. It was the second house he'd owned. The first had been sold five years ago after his divorce, when he realized the memories that resided there were too painful to avoid.

He'd bought this particular house for a song because of all the work it needed. He'd thought it would be a terrific project in his spare time, a hobby to keep painful thoughts at bay.

As always when he entered the foyer a faint sense of satisfaction swept over him. The wooden floor gleamed beneath his feet and the throw rug in shades of copper and brown emphasized the beauty of the wood beneath.

He tossed his keys on the small table in the hallway and went directly up the stairs to the master bedroom.

He'd give himself a couple of hours of sleep and then head into the office to see if anything had popped.

It took him only minutes to place his gun and holster on the nightstand and undress and get into bed. Even though he was exhausted, his mind refused to turn off as it replayed the events of the day. He believed Peyton's story of what had happened, but he'd still instructed Sam to run background checks on both Peyton and Rick. The last thing he wanted was for something unexpected to jump up and bite him on the butt.

Every base needed to be covered, and he was certain as he closed his eyes that he'd covered them all. They were a small town, with a small force of law enforcement officers, but Tom was confident in his team. They were all smart and committed to their work.

As sleep began to edge in, his thoughts turned to Peyton. She'd touched him on levels nobody had reached in a very long time. She had to be strong in order to have survived her childhood, and yet there was that frailty about her that made him want to take care of her.

If he were completely honest with himself, he had to acknowledge that as he'd held her in his arms he'd been stunned to realize that although his intent had been to comfort, there had been a part of him, a strictly male part, that had enjoyed the feel of her in his arms.

In fact, he had more than enjoyed it. A quick fire of desire had swept through him as he'd felt the press of her soft breasts against his chest, as he'd smelled the fresh scent of her hair. It had stunned him, first because it was so unexpected and second because it was inappropriate, considering the circumstances.

He drifted asleep with thoughts of her in his head and awoke to his alarm clock ringing two hours later. He rolled over and punched it off, then bounded out of bed, eager to get to the office and find out how things had gone while he'd been sleeping. A sense of urgency chased him. Somewhere out there was a baby who needed to be brought home.

He was in the office by seven-thirty, and Sam greeted him as he walked through the door. Sam McCain was a big, burly black man who had come to Black Rock after working as a policeman in Chicago. He and his wife had moved there for the slower pace and a safer place to raise their kids.

Every day Tom was thankful that Sam had landed here working for him. "Hey, Sam. Please tell me the phone has been ringing off the wall with tips on Lilly Wilkerson's whereabouts."

Sam frowned and shook his head. "We've only had two calls so far this morning, and if you think real hard you'll be able to tell me who they were from."

"Sally Bernard called threatening to kill her husband, and Walt Toliver called to report that Lilly was probably taken into the spaceship that landed in his field last night," Tom replied.

"And the kewpie doll goes to the big fella with the gun on his hip," Sam exclaimed.

Tom grinned. "It wouldn't be a normal day without the two of them calling in." His grin flattened into a frown. "I was really hoping somebody would have seen this Kathy Simon."

"It's early yet, boss. It's possible she's holed up somewhere for the night, but eventually she'll have to get out and around, and somebody will see her."

"Where's Brittany?"

"She hasn't shown up yet," Sam replied.

Tom looked at his watch. She should have been in a half an hour ago. "Has she called in?" Sam shook his head. Tom sighed. "This is the third time in the last couple of weeks that she's been late. Guess I'm going to have to kick some sister butt."

Sam grinned. "Benjamin called earlier to tell you that everything is under control at the Wilkerson house and Caleb is waiting for you in your office."

"As soon as I check a few things here I'll be heading back over there," Tom said as he walked to his office.

Caleb sat in the chair in front of Tom's desk, his big feet propped up on the polished oak. Tom slapped Caleb's legs as he passed by and frowned in disapproval. His younger brother hurriedly straightened up.

"You heard from Brittany this morning?" he asked Caleb as he eased down into the chair at his desk.

"Why would I hear from her?" Caleb asked.

"She's late…again."

"She's probably hung over. She's spending way too much time down at Harley's bar. I think she has a crush on the new bartender there."

"I don't care what she does in her time off, but I can't have her ambling into work whenever she feels like it."

Tom definitely needed to have a stern conversation with his baby sister. "But in the meantime, I'm headed back over to the Wilkerson place to check on Peyton."

Caleb frowned. "Don't you find it odd that nobody saw this woman who supposedly stole her baby? She didn't know where this Kathy lived, doesn't have a picture of the woman and doesn't have any evidence to support that this woman even exists."

"Do you have pictures of your friends?" Tom countered. "Peyton only knew Kathy for two months, a span of time when Peyton wasn't taking her baby out much. Odd? Maybe. But impossible to believe? No."

"I think you should order that new patio ripped up," Caleb said. "I think if you want to find that baby then that's the first place you should look."

"I'll tell you what you're going to do today," Tom said. "According to Peyton, this Kathy Simon has been in town for at least two months. During that time she had to eat, so I want you to spend the day taking a sketch to every grocery store and every restaurant in town and find out who saw her when."

"Sounds like a waste of time," Caleb exclaimed.

"Your time is mine as long as you wear that deputy badge, little brother. Oh, and another thing, apparently Peyton had a run-in with somebody in the parking lot of the grocery store last week. She said the guy was driving a black pickup and had shaggy brown hair. See if you can figure out who that might have been."

"Now, that sounds like a bunch of busy work," Caleb exclaimed.

Tom smiled. "So get out of here and get busy."

As Caleb left, Tom called Sam into his office. "Coordinate with the others and start a door-to-door campaign to find somebody who knew Kathy Simon. I'm headed to the victim's house. Keep me updated on any calls that come in, anything that smells just a little bit like a break."

"Got it," Sam replied and followed Tom out of his office.

"Oh, one more thing. Call Brittany and tell her to get her butt in here, and call the men off the roadblocks. My guess is that Kathy Simon scooted out of town as fast as she could and is probably long gone."

Minutes later, as Tom drove toward Peyton's house, he wondered what condition she'd be in when he arrived. Although he didn't know personally what it was like to have a kidnapped child, he certainly knew personally how to grieve for a child.

His head filled with a vision of a baby face with merry brown eyes and chubby cheeks. Even though it had been five years since he'd lost her, his heart constricted with pain.

Nobody should have to suffer the loss of a child, and he certainly didn't want Peyton to know that kind of pain. She was hurting now, but if her baby wasn't returned to her and all hope was lost, she would be cast into a hollow darkness that Tom knew too well.

But he couldn't think about his own loss. He needed to focus on making sure that everything was being done to bring baby Lilly home. He also needed to decide if the FBI needed to be called in. At the moment, his plan was to give himself and his deputies twenty-four more hours to find Kathy Simon. If they didn't succeed, then they would have to proceed under the assumption that Kathy Simon had crossed state lines with the kidnapped infant.

Rick's car was back in Peyton's driveway as Tom parked at the curb. Benjamin's car was also still there. It was Benjamin who opened the door to his knock. He looked tired.

"Heard anything?" he asked Tom.

"Nothing. How are things here?"

"A bit tense. She didn't sleep much, hasn't eaten at all. Rick showed up about an hour ago and they're in the kitchen now."

Tom clapped his brother on the shoulder. "Go home. Get some sleep."

As Benjamin headed out the door Tom walked toward the kitchen where the murmurs of Peyton and Rick's voices drifted out.

"Tom!" Peyton jumped up from the table as he entered the room, looking relieved to see him.

"I hope you've brought us some news," Rick said. He started to rise as well, but Tom motioned him back into his chair.

"Unfortunately, I don't have news," Tom said, hating the way the hopeful expression on Peyton's face fell away. "The roadblocks on either end of town yielded nothing."

"She had plenty of time to get out of town before you

put those roadblocks into effect," Rick replied. "Peyton isn't even sure how long she was unconscious. She might have had as much as a half an hour head start before Peyton called for help."

"I'm aware of that," Tom replied. He leaned against the kitchen counter and tried not to notice how Peyton's jeans hugged the long length of her legs, how the blue T-shirt she wore perfectly matched her eyes and molded to the full breasts that had been against his chest the night before.

He focused his attention on Rick. "We're starting door-to-door canvassing this morning, hoping somebody knows something about Kathy Simon. She was in town for at least two months. She had to be living somewhere, and if we can find out where that was, then maybe we can get some clue as to where she might have gone."

Rick nodded. He looked tired, as if the night had been unkind to him and sleep had not come easy. "I just hope we get her back today. I hate to leave here without everything being resolved."

Tom focused again on Peyton. "How are you holding up?" His heart squeezed in his chest as he saw the dark smudges beneath her eyes, the lines of strain on either side of her mouth.

"I'm okay." She lifted her chin, but the defiant gesture only added to her fragile appearance.

"I'd like to hand out some flyers," Rick said. "I'll go stir crazy if I have to sit around here all day."

"If you go to the sheriff's office on Main, my deputy

Sam McCain can give you some flyers to pass out," Tom said.

Rick cast Peyton a worried look. "You'll be okay if I leave?"

"Of course." She sat back down at the table and curled her slender fingers around a mug of coffee.

"Have you eaten anything?" Tom asked Peyton the minute Rick had left the house.

She waved a hand in dismissal. "I'm not hungry."

"You have to eat," Tom said firmly. "You're running on nothing but nerves and energy, and that will make you sick." He went to the refrigerator and pulled out a package of bacon and a carton of eggs. "Now point to where you keep your skillet." She pointed to a lower cabinet and Tom got to work.

"I've racked my brain trying to think of something Kathy might have said to me about her past, but I can't think of anything concrete. I just feel like with every minute that passes Lilly gets farther away from me."

Tom searched for a response that would give her hope but wouldn't sound like a meaningless platitude. He continued to search for positive things to say to her as the day wore on and little news came in.

What bothered Tom most was that Kathy Simon had seemingly managed to drift around town for the last two months like a ghost, with nobody seeing her and nobody interacting with her.

Except Peyton.

And as the day wore on Peyton's emotions grew more raw, more difficult for Tom to witness.

As evening approached, Rick returned to the house to check in before he headed back to Wichita.

"We have flyers up all over town," Rick said as he raked a hand through his hair. "Surely somebody who sees them will know something and come forward."

"God, I hope so," Peyton exclaimed.

"As much as I hate to leave, I've got to get back to Wichita," Rick said, his gaze going first to Peyton and then to Tom. "I'm sorry. I don't know what else to do."

"Go, Rick. There's nothing more you can do for now," Peyton replied.

"You'll call me with any news?" he asked Tom.

"Absolutely."

With a nod to Tom, Rick left the house.

When he left, Peyton turned to Tom, her eyes filled with an agony he felt in his own chest.

"I can't believe it's going to be night again and we're no closer to finding her than we were last night." She stuffed the back of her hand against her mouth as if to keep a sob from escaping.

Tom wanted to take her into his arms but didn't, perhaps because he wanted too badly to hold her once again. Instead, at that moment his cell phone rang.

"Sheriff Grayson," he answered.

"Tom, it's Jack Warner. The missus and me just got back from spending a couple of days with our boy in Kansas City. I just saw one of those flyers you're circulating around town. You know that garage apartment I rent behind my house? Well, I believe the woman you're looking for is renting it, except she rented it by the name of Sarah Johnson. She's been here about two months. Her car is there now if you want to get over here."

Tom's heartbeat kicked up a thousand notches. "You sure it's the same woman?"

"If it's not, then it's her twin."

"Thanks, Jack. Do me a favor, stay away from the apartment and I'll be right there." He hung up and looked at Peyton, who was staring at him with a glimmer of hope shining from her eyes.

"I think we might have an address for Kathy Simon," he said.

She was out of the chair and at the door to the kitchen before the words had completely left his mouth. "Let's go."

He hesitated. He wasn't sure why, but he had a bad feeling. "I think it would be best if you stay here."

"Yeah, right." Without waiting for his reply, she headed for the front door.

As Tom followed behind her he hoped that his bad feeling was nothing more than heartburn.

Chapter 4

The thrum of excitement that filled Peyton was almost as sickening as the helpless, hopeless feeling that had been with her all day long.

"Four years ago, Jack Warner and his wife renovated their detached garage and made it into a small studio apartment," Tom said. "Their son rented it from them until he got married and moved into his own house, and since then they've rented it out to whoever needed it. Jack told me a woman by the name of Sarah Johnson rented it and has been living there for the past two months. He said Sarah Johnson looks exactly like the woman on our flyers."

"So, she used a fake name to rent the place. Surely we'll find something there that will give us a clue to her real identity," Peyton said. "A fingerprint or maybe something she left behind." Excitement roared through her. "We're a step closer, Tom. We're a step closer to having Lilly back where she belongs."

He frowned, and with that gesture some of Peyton's excitement waned. "What's wrong?" she asked. "What is it you aren't telling me?"

"Jack said her car is parked out front. I'm trying to figure out why a woman who snatched a baby didn't take her car when she left town."

A faint disquiet swept through Peyton. "Maybe she was afraid we'd find out about the car and could broadcast the license plate information with the AMBER Alert?"

"Maybe, but then the question becomes how did she leave town? There's no bus service in Black Rock, no airport or train station."

"Maybe she didn't leave town. Maybe she's crazy enough to think that she could steal my baby and stay in that garage apartment and nobody would know." Even as Peyton said the words, she didn't believe them.

It didn't make sense. But then nothing had made sense since the moment Kathy had attacked her in the bathroom.

"She'd be stupid to hang around here," Tom replied. "And a woman who was able to so thoroughly manipulate you and plan Lilly's kidnapping wouldn't be stupid enough to hang around town."

"So, she'd have to have an accomplice, somebody working with her." The idea that there might be two people who had wanted her baby was almost as frightening as anything else that had happened so far.

"Maybe a husband or a boyfriend," Tom said.

"How could a man allow himself to be a party to such a crime?" she asked.

Tom shot her a quick glance as he turned off Main Street and onto a tree-studded residential road. "My brothers and I call that crazy love."

"Crazy love?"

He nodded. "You see it in the headlines all the time. A woman who helps her husband kidnap women for his sexual pleasure. She does it because she loves him. Or a man who might help his wife run a credit card scam because he loves her too much to tell her no."

"That's not crazy love. That's two crazy people thinking what they feel is love," she replied.

"You wouldn't break the law for a man you loved?" he asked.

A nervous laugh escaped her. "I'd never be with a man who would ask me to break the law," she replied.

"That's good to know," he replied.

Every muscle in her body tensed as Tom pulled the car to the curb in front of a neat ranch house. An older man sat on a wicker chair on the front porch and rose to his feet at the sight of them.

Tom unfastened his seat belt and then turned and looked at her. "Peyton, I need you to stay in the car until I assess the scene. I don't want to put you in danger, and I certainly don't want to put your baby in danger if she's somewhere on the property."

Although she desperately wanted to be beside him when he went into the apartment, she reluctantly nodded her head. The last thing she would want to do was put Lilly at any greater risk.

"I don't want to make things more difficult for you." She placed a hand on his forearm. "But, if Lilly's in there and you get to her, you'll bring her right to me, yes?" Her heart beat loudly in her ears and she felt half-breathless with anxiety.

"Of course, but you know, Peyton, the likelihood of them being here is pretty low."

She squeezed his arm. "Just go find something, Tom. Find something that will get my baby back in my arms." She released her hold on him and watched as he got out of the car and met the man she assumed was Jack Warner in the middle of the front yard. She quickly rolled down her window so she could hear the conversation taking place between the two.

"She was no trouble at all," Jack said to Tom. "Paid the rent in cash on time and kept to herself. I never saw anyone here visiting her."

"Did you have her fill out a background form before renting to her?"

Jack laughed and shook his head. "Now, Tom, you know that's not how we do things here in Black Rock. She seemed like a nice young woman and she had the cash in hand. She told us she wanted a fresh start and had fallen in love with Black Rock. That was good enough for me and Martha."

"Did she mention where she was from?"

Jack frowned. "I don't believe it came up." As the two men began to walk around the side of the house, their voices were lost to Peyton.

She unfastened her seat belt and tried to still the frantic pounding of her heart. Even though she knew it was completely irrational, she hoped and prayed that Tom would open up that apartment door and Kathy would be sitting on her sofa with Lilly on her lap.

Closing her eyes, she imagined Lilly in her mind. Her head filled with the sweet baby scent of her daughter, and a vision of Lilly's toothless smile nearly made her cry out loud.

She felt as if she'd been so strong, had tried so hard to keep it all together, but at the moment she felt as if the smallest thing could shatter her completely apart.

All she could do was pray that wherever Lilly was, she was safe and with somebody who was loving her and taking care of her until the time she was back in Peyton's arms.

One thing was certain. She was grateful for Tom. His calm, steady presence through all of this was part of what had kept her sane. All she had to do was look in his dark brown eyes and she felt the calm soothing her rising hysteria.

The hours spent with Rick had only reconfirmed the fact that they hadn't been right for each other. Although he'd tried to be supportive in his own way and she knew he was hurting, too, she'd almost been grateful when he'd gone back to Wichita.

It wasn't lost on Peyton that she'd found comfort

in Tom's arms and not in Lilly's father's arms. On some level it surprised her to realize that she felt more comfortable with the handsome sheriff than she had in all the months of her relationship with Rick.

Rick was self-contained, rarely showing any deep emotion. He was a bundle of suppressed energy. All qualities that she knew made him a wonderful assistant district attorney but didn't bode well for personal relationships.

Tom was different. She sensed a tremendous capacity for love in him. It shone from his eyes when he spoke of his family, and it had radiated from his very being when he'd held her in his arms.

She sighed with impatience. She knew what she was doing—thinking of anything and everything except what might be taking place in the apartment where Kathy Simon had lived.

What was taking so long? Why hadn't Tom come out to tell her what he'd found? With each agonizing minute that ticked by, it became more apparent to her that Lilly wasn't inside the apartment.

Something was wrong. She felt it in the sudden weight of her heart in her chest. Something was wrong and she needed to know what it was, what was happening. She needed to know right now.

Even though she'd told Tom she'd remain in the car and stay out of his way, the need to get out of the car and go to the garage apartment was stronger than her half-hearted commitment to Tom to stay in the car.

She opened the car door and got out, a terrible

foreboding washing over her. It was taking too long. Something just wasn't right.

As she began to walk toward the side of the house where Tom and Jack had disappeared, she felt as if her feet were weighed down by the inexplicable dread that coursed through her.

When she reached the side of the house, the detached garage came into view. Two things caused a screaming alarm to go off in her head. The first was Jack Warner seated on the grass next to the building with his hands over his face. The second was Tom standing off to one side talking frantically into his cell phone.

Tom's features were taut with tension, and that tension electrified Peyton. A screaming protest came from her. Then she whispered, "No." Suddenly she was running, deep sobs welling up inside her as she raced for the open front door.

"Peyton, wait! Don't go in there," Tom exclaimed.

She ignored him. She ran into the front door and stopped short as a deep moan escaped her. On the floor just inside the door was Kathy Simon. Dead.

The young woman was sprawled on her back like a broken doll. Her blue eyes were wide open and staring up as if in surprise. Her hair was no longer long and red but instead was cut short and dyed black. Still, there was no question it was Kathy.

A large knife protruded from her chest.

"Oh, God. Oh, God," Peyton gasped. "Lilly!" The name ripped from the depths of her being as she nearly fell to her knees.

"Peyton." Tom gripped her firmly by one arm. "She's not here. Listen to me, Peyton. I promise you Lilly isn't here. You need to come outside now. This is an active crime scene."

She stared up at him with incomprehension but allowed him to lead her back outside, where she drew several deep, steadying breaths. "I don't understand. Who would do this? What's going on? And where is my baby, Tom?"

"I don't know, Peyton," he replied.

For the first time since Lilly had disappeared, Peyton faced the possibility that she might never see her daughter again.

Tom stepped outside the garage apartment and drew a deep, weary sigh. It was just after midnight and the scene had been processed. Kathy's body had been taken away to be looked at more thoroughly by the local medical examiner.

Peyton had left the scene hours earlier. Benjamin had taken her home and was staying with her so Tom could sort things out there.

The medical examiner had tentatively determined that death had probably occurred sometime the evening before. Cause of death had been the single deep stab wound to the chest.

Tom now not only had the job of finding Lilly but also of solving a murder. The only sign that Lilly had been in the studio apartment at all was a tiny pink bootie he'd found next to the sofa.

He drew in a deep breath of the hot night air as his brain worked overtime to try to make sense of everything. Why would somebody murder a kidnapper? And where had Lilly been taken?

Caleb stepped outside and joined Tom. "We found her purse in the closet. She's got a driver's license in the name of Kathy Simon and another in the name of Sarah Johnson. To my eyes they both look like very good fakes."

Tom frowned. "We'll run her fingerprints through the AFIS system and see if anything pops." He knew it could take anywhere from twenty-four to forty-eight hours for the Automated Fingerprint Identification System to make a match and that was only if she'd been arrested or had her fingerprints taken in the past.

"Maybe with a real identification it will be easier to make sense of all this," Caleb said. "I'm glad you didn't rip up Peyton's patio looking for a body. Guess I was off base where she's concerned."

Tom clapped a hand on his brother's shoulder. "You were right to be suspicious of Peyton's story." He dropped his arm back to his side. "What a mess."

"I hate to add to the mess, but nobody's heard from Brittany all day," Caleb said. "I drove by her place on my way here, and her car is gone."

"God, I hope she hasn't gone and done something stupid." Tom released another deep sigh. "I suppose she'll eventually call one of us." He would be more concerned if Brittany hadn't done this before.

Brittany was only eighteen when their parents had

died, and despite the support of her brothers, she'd taken the deaths hard.

Tom had been thrilled when she'd decided to follow her brothers' footsteps and make her career law enforcement. She was not only beautiful, but she was also exceptionally bright and had become a valuable team player in the Black Rock Sheriff's Department. Unfortunately, far too often her personal life interfered with her professional one.

"I'm going to have to talk to her. I can't let her just disappear every time she gets a new boyfriend or feels like she needs some time alone. If she's going to work for me, then I have to know I can depend on her," Tom said.

"Don't be too hard on her. She's just having trouble growing up," Caleb replied.

"In the meantime, I've got a murder to solve and a baby to find," Tom replied. His thoughts turned to Peyton. She had to be hysterical over this latest turn of events.

He wished he had the time to go over to her house, to somehow find the right words to assuage her fears, but he didn't. He didn't have the right words and he didn't have the time.

He and his deputies needed to go over the crime scene again and canvass the neighborhood to see if anyone had seen anything related to the murder.

Besides, it bothered him that he wanted to be there for her, that all he could think about was how badly she needed to be held right now.

It had been a very long time since he'd had any interest in a woman. Five years earlier, his heart had been ripped out of his chest and he'd thought the wound was fatal, that he'd never feel anything for another woman again.

Peyton was the first woman since the tragedy to make him feel again, and he didn't like it. The last thing he wanted was to get close to a woman, to fall in love again.

He raked a hand down his face, inwardly cursing his own foolishness. The only interest Peyton had in him was as a lawman who could bring her baby home. But he couldn't do that until they got an ID on the dead woman in Jack Warner's apartment.

They worked through the night. The fingerprints lifted were sent to a lab in Topeka, along with any other forensic evidence they'd collected. Black Rock was far too small to have anything resembling a crime lab, so they used the lab in Topeka.

Sam was dispatched to physically drive the evidence to Topeka, although the fingerprints were already being run through the AFIS. Neighbors were contacted and statements were taken, but nobody had seen anything that might give a clue to the killer.

The evidence pointed to Kathy Simon opening her door to her killer. There was no sign of forced entry at any of the doors or windows.

Tom could only speculate on why Kathy had stayed in town, and his theory was that somebody—a partner— had met her there and she had planned to leave with that person. Not only had her hair been cut and dyed, but a suitcase containing all of her clothes had been packed and was waiting in the closet.

She'd been ready to run, but why had she waited so long? Waiting for her accomplice to show up? There was no way to know if that accomplice was male or female. Was it somebody from Kathy's life before she moved here or somebody here in town?

He hated to think that it was somebody in his town, a friend or neighbor who smiled at him or raised a hand in greeting but secretly had the capacity for kidnapping and murder.

It was after six in the morning when Tom finally headed to Peyton's place. He wished he had something to give her, but he had nothing. His men were out canvassing the streets, the evidence was on its way to the lab and so far there had been nothing from the AFIS.

He'd sent photos of the victim to all the news sources hoping that somebody would see the photo on the news and be able to make an official identification.

It was a waiting game…waiting for the physical evidence to turn up something, waiting to see if her fingerprints would identify her. Until they knew her real name, he had no idea in what direction to take the investigation.

As he parked in Peyton's driveway, the sun appeared in the eastern sky, promising another hot, clear day. He was exhausted but felt he owed it to Peyton to stop by and check in with her.

Wearily he pulled himself out of his car, wishing he

had something to tell Peyton that would bring a smile to her face, irritated with himself by how badly he wanted to see a smile from her.

When he reached the front door he knocked softly and Benjamin answered. "How's she doing?" Tom asked as he stepped into the small foyer.

"She napped on and off during the night. She's been real quiet, very self-contained." Benjamin frowned. "And I'm assuming there's nothing new."

"Nothing," Tom replied. "Hopefully by the end of the day we'll have a good identification and can go from there. Where is Peyton now?"

"She's in the nursery."

"Go home, get some sleep, I might need you later today," Tom said.

Benjamin nodded and Tom clapped him on the shoulder. "I'll talk to you later," Tom said.

He stood at the door and watched as Benjamin got into his car and drove off, wishing he could go in and tell Peyton something positive, but he had nothing to offer her. As he went down the hallway toward the nursery, the silence of the house pressed in around him. He summoned what strength he had left to face Peyton.

He stepped into the doorway of the nursery and found her sitting in a rocking chair facing the window. She wasn't aware of his presence, and for a moment he merely stood, his breath stuck in his chest as he looked at her.

The morning sun caught in her hair and sparkled with a thousand pinpoints of light. There was no question that something about this woman resonated deep inside him. It wasn't just her physical beauty that fired through him, that was a given.

It was more than that. It was a need to right her world, a desire to be a hero for her. It was like nothing he'd felt before, and it scared him more than just a little bit.

"Peyton." He spoke her name softly, not wanting to startle her.

She swiveled the rocker around to face him, and his heart nearly broke. She clutched to her chest a pink teddy bear and her tired eyes held all the sorrow of the universe.

"Nothing?" she said, her voice a mere whisper as she motioned him into an overstuffed chair in the corner.

"We're working on getting an identification from her fingerprints. Once we know who she is and where she's from we'll be much closer to finding Lilly." He sat in the chair, wishing he had more for her.

She rocked for a moment, the chair squeaking slightly with each back-and-forth motion. "Despite what she did, she didn't deserve to die that way," she finally said. She stopped rocking and her eyes were midnight-blue as she looked at him. "It was awful. I can't get the imagine of her on the floor out of my head."

"I know. I'm sorry you saw it," he replied.

"You look exhausted. You shouldn't be here. You should be home getting some sleep," she said.

"I didn't want to go home before stopping by here to talk to you," he replied.

She turned and looked back out the window, the

rocking chair once again creaking with her movement. His eyes felt gritty with lack of sleep, and the longer he sat in the chair the heavier his body became.

This felt familiar, this intense desire to fix things, to somehow make sense of tragedy, the need to comfort a woman's pain.

"I had a child once." The words fell out of his mouth before he'd realized they were even in his thoughts. She turned once again to look at him, a quizzical and cautious look in her eyes.

"You said *had*," she said softly.

He nodded. "Her name was Kelly. My wife used to like to call her Kelly belly." Emotion pressed tight against his chest. He hadn't intended to talk about this, had spent the last five years of his life trying not to think about it. "She was two when we lost her."

He stared past her and out the window, but in his mind's eye he saw a chubby little girl with laughing brown eyes and tousled dark curls. The pain he'd once felt when thinking about Kelly wasn't as sharp as it had been, although he would always ache for the child he'd lost.

"What happened?" Peyton's voice pulled him back to the present.

"I was at work when it happened. My wife, Julie, had taken Kelly out in the front yard to play. Kelly was already a handful. She never talked if she could sing, never walked if she could run." He felt the smile that curved his lips for just a moment and then felt it fall away.

"It happened in the split second of a heartbeat," he continued. "Julie looked away, Kelly took off running and the driver in the car coming down the street never saw her."

He heard Peyton's gasp and he smiled and shook his head. "She died instantly. Six months later, Julie left me. She couldn't forgive herself even though I told her there was nothing to forgive, that it had been a tragic accident. But she told me she couldn't look at me, that it was just too painful for her to be with me, and so we divorced."

"Oh, Tom, I'm so sorry." She got up from the rocking chair and placed the teddy bear in the crib.

He knew he should stand and go home, but the weariness that suddenly swept over him made any movement near impossible. "I didn't tell you this to make you feel sorry for me," he said as she walked closer to where he sat. "I just wanted you to know that I know what it's like to miss a child."

To his surprise she sat on his lap, curled her arms around his neck and laid her head on his chest. He wrapped his arms around her and held tight.

There was nothing sexual in the embrace—they were simply two parents grieving for what might be and what would never be.

With the sweet scent of her hair in his head and the warmth of her arms around his neck, Tom closed his eyes and prayed that she would never know the finality of loss that he experienced every day of his life.

Chapter 5

"India Richards," Tom said to Peyton that evening. He'd left her place that morning and had gone home to get some much-needed sleep and arrived back at her house a few minutes after five. "Does that name ring a bell?"

Peyton shook her head. "That's who she was?" She motioned him onto the sofa, glad to see he looked rested.

Even with the drama and uncertainty in her life at the moment, she wasn't oblivious to the fact that there was something crazy between them, a connection on some level she'd never felt before with another person.

"Not only that, but she had a rap sheet as long as my arm," he said as he eased down on the sofa cushion.

"Seriously?" Peyton sat in the chair facing him and

remembered how his arms had felt around her that morning, how somehow their pain had mingled together and become more tolerable.

"Nothing violent. Three years ago she was charged with shoplifting and petty theft in Kansas City, also a prostitution charge there. She got off on probation each time, then apparently moved to Wichita and two years ago was charged with shoplifting once again."

"Wichita. So she might have seen me and Lilly there, possibly followed us here to Black Rock." The thought of being singled out and stalked sent a chill up Peyton's spine. "Do you know where she lived in Wichita?"

"Last known address was on Grand Road."

Peyton frowned. "That's clear on the other side of town, miles from where I lived."

"Maybe she saw you in a grocery store. Maybe you shared the same hairdresser or dental office. You could have run into her in a million places and not known it. Now that we know her name, we're working with the authorities in Wichita to find out everything we can about her. Hopefully they can tell us who she associated with and from there we can figure out who might have had reason to kill her. In the meantime, news agencies are requesting anyone with information regarding India to contact my office or the authorities in Wichita. I've also sent Caleb to Wichita to do some investigating."

"So hopefully somebody will come forward with information that will lead us to Lilly," she said.

"That's what we want, Peyton. That's what everyone wants. Have you heard from Rick?"

She nodded. "He's been calling about every two hours to see if there's any progress. He's worried sick."

"He should be here with you," Tom replied.

She heard the faint edge of scorn in his voice and smiled. "To be perfectly honest, he wanted to drive out, but I discouraged him. There's nothing he can do here but pace my living room floor and make me even more on edge than I already am. I don't need him here."

It was a bit unsettling for her to realize she'd known Tom for less than a week and yet he was the one she wanted to be with her, to support her.

She knew better than to trust her feelings where Tom was concerned. She was certain that it was the situation that had her feeling so close to him. After all, he was the man she was depending on to bring her baby home. The fact that he'd told her about his wife and baby girl had made her feel even closer to him.

"Do you want some coffee or something?" she asked. She got up from the chair, needing to do something to take her mind off her growing feelings for a man she barely knew and the ticking of the clock racing down to another night without Lilly in her arms.

"Coffee would be good," he agreed.

He followed her into the kitchen, where she busied herself making the coffee while he sat at the table. She'd been so strong through the day, but as the sun dipped in the western skies anxiety and grief began to build inside her. Like a scream waiting to be released.

She poured the coffee and joined him at the table.

"Now our goal is to try to retrace India's footsteps

before this all occurred. There's obviously somebody else involved in the kidnapping," Tom said. He took a sip of his coffee and eyed her over the rim of the cup. "Are you sure there's nobody else from your past that might want to hurt you? Did you date anyone before Rick? Somebody who might not have been happy that you hooked up with Rick and had a baby?"

"I only dated one other man before Rick. He was a waiter at one of the restaurants I worked at. We dated off and on for two years, then I met Rick."

"What's his name?"

"Cliff Gunther, but I can't imagine him having anything to do with this," she protested, then frowned. "But, I also couldn't imagine Kathy doing anything like this."

"When was the last time you saw him?" he asked.

"Just before I moved here. I went to visit him at the restaurant where he worked and told him I was moving."

"What restaurant?" Tom asked.

"Henry's Italian Cuisine in Wichita."

At that moment Tom's phone rang.

Peyton immediately felt the tension that wafted off him. He shot her a glance, then rose from the table and carried the phone into the living room. She stared after him, fear piercing through her. Who was he talking to, and why had he felt the need to leave the room? *Don't let it be something terrible about Lilly,* she prayed.

Her heart thundered in her chest painfully fast, and for a moment she couldn't breathe. *Had somebody found*

Lilly? Had something bad happened? Was Lilly dead?
The thoughts crashed through her brain, the kind of
thoughts that no mother should ever have in her head.
She only breathed again when Tom stepped back into
the kitchen. "What is it? Has something happened?"
she asked.

"I've got to leave," he replied, his features without
expression.

Peyton jumped up from her chair. "Tom, what's
happened?" The scream she'd been fighting against
for the past two days rose up in the back of her throat.
"Is Lilly dead?" The dreadful words yanked out of the
very depths of her.

"No. No!" He grabbed her by the shoulders. "That's
not what the phone call was about."

"Then what?" She stepped away from him. "I know
it was about the case. You have to tell me."

He hesitated, the frown once again digging into his
forehead. "We got a tip from a woman who says her
neighbors have a new infant. They told the neighbor
it's an adopted baby, but the neighbor is suspicious. The
couple lives in Laville, a little town about thirty minutes
north of here."

"And you're going there to check it out?" she asked.
"Then I'm coming with you," she said as he nodded.

"Peyton, this could very well be a wild-goose chase,"
he protested. "It could be nothing more than a waste of
time."

"I have plenty of time to waste," she replied. There
was no way she wasn't going to be in that car with him

when he went to check it out. "Please don't fight with me, Tom. I can either ride with you in your car or I'll be following behind you in mine, but one way or another, I'm going along."

"I don't want you getting your hopes up," he said moments later as he backed out of her driveway. She'd brought along Lilly's car seat, which was now buckled into the back of the patrol car. "It's possible we're going to get a lot of tips that are going to be without merit."

"And I'll be hopeful with each tip that comes in," she replied. "I don't know how to be anything else."

They drove for a few minutes in silence. Even though Peyton knew he was right, that she was a fool to get her hopes up, she couldn't help the wild hope that filled her at the possibility that they could be driving to a sweet reunion with her baby.

She had to continue to believe that Lilly was going to be returned to her safe and sound. Any other thought was too horrible to consider.

"You're the strongest woman I've ever met," he said, breaking the silence. "No matter what happens, I want you to know that I admire the way you've handled yourself through all this."

"Blame it on my childhood. Surviving that took a healthy dose of strength." She stared out the side window, infused with painful memories of her past. "It's ironic. My mother did everything wrong to assure that I would survive my youth. I've tried to do everything right, and look where we are."

"You can't blame yourself for what's happened with Lilly."

"I don't." It was true. Peyton didn't blame herself. "I trusted a woman I thought was a friend. I had no way of knowing she wasn't who she presented herself to be. If I blame myself for that then I'll never trust anyone in my life again."

"And that would be the real tragedy in all this," he replied.

"Why haven't you remarried, Tom?" she asked. She couldn't imagine that it had been for lack of female interest.

He was hot, and more than that he seemed to be kind and sensitive. He was the total package, and she couldn't believe that all the single women in Black Rock hadn't noticed.

"Just not interested," he replied. "Until the accident it was pretty good. Sure, Julie and I had some issues, no marriage is perfect, but for the most part it was all pretty good. I just don't want to do it again. It's as simple as that."

"So, you don't believe in second chances at happiness?"

He shot her a quick glance. "I can be happy and single. Besides, I've got a big family, it's not like I'll ever be lonely." He turned off the main highway and onto a county road.

"I want to be married," she replied. "I feel like I've been alone all my life and I can't wait to find that special man to share the rest of my life with me."

They fell silent once again, and the rise of anxiety pressed tight against Peyton's chest. She needed Lilly. She couldn't imagine having to spend the rest of her life with the kind of grief that Tom lived with, with the ache of a child lost forever.

As they got closer to the address Tom had been given, he felt Peyton's hope fill the car, and he was sorry she was with him, afraid that if the infant wasn't Lilly then the composure that Peyton had maintained for so long would finally crack.

He'd been a fool to let her come along. He shouldn't have told her what the phone call had been about. This wasn't just about finding out if Lilly was there; it was possible they were going to the home of India's murderer. Having Peyton along with him was not only unprofessional, but it could also be dangerous.

He glanced over where she stared out the window. There was no question that he found her more attractive than he'd found any woman in years. Her blond hair fell to her shoulders in a soft wave, and even the worry that furrowed her brow couldn't diminish her beauty.

He was compromising his professional ethics by allowing her to be with him and wondered why he was having such a problem keeping his personal feelings out of this case.

He'd always found it easy to maintain a professional distance, an emotional detachment on the cases he worked as sheriff. In the years he'd been in charge he'd had to occasionally arrest people he thought of as friends, he'd had to investigate neighbors and never had he allowed his personal feelings about the matter get in the way of his duty.

Maybe it was because this case was about Lilly. Maybe it was impossible to separate himself from Peyton's emotions because in many ways they were so close to his own.

He tightened his grip on the steering wheel as he turned down a dirt road that would take him to the farmhouse they sought.

He was familiar with the area, as it was part of his jurisdiction, although he didn't know the people who lived in the particular house where they were going.

"Peyton, you have to wait in the car while I check it out," he said. "That's not a suggestion, it's a command. You can't forget that somebody murdered India and we don't know if one of the people in this farmhouse is responsible for her death. I need you to stay in the car to assure your own personal safety, but more importantly it might assure Lilly's personal safety if she's in there."

She looked at him with her amazing blue eyes and offered him a nervous half smile. "I won't do anything to jeopardize Lilly's safety. As difficult as it will be for me, I'll wait in the car until you tell me to get out."

He nodded. "I appreciate your cooperation."

She released a small sigh. "I want it to be her so badly I feel sick."

He fought the impulse to reach over and cover her hand with his. Somehow he had to stop wanting to touch her all the time. Eventually this case would end, hopefully with a happy ending, and she could move on with her life and find a man who wanted to marry and spend forever with her.

He definitely wasn't that man.

He pulled to the side of the road and shut off the engine. "What are you doing?" Peyton asked.

"Benjamin is meeting me here. I didn't want to go in without backup," he replied. He could tell that this information frightened her.

She needed to be frightened. There was no assurance that there wasn't danger in coming here.

By the time Benjamin pulled up behind them, Tom wasn't sure whether it was her tension that filled the car or his own.

He got out of the car and met his brother, who had gotten out of his own vehicle. "This might be nothing but a wild-goose chase," he said to Benjamin. "Maybe a neighbor with a beef blowing a whistle on an innocent set of new adoptive parents."

Benjamin flashed Tom a tight smile. "Won't be the first wild-goose chase we've shared."

"Be ready for anything. I don't know what we're walking into. Somebody put a six-inch blade into India Richards's heart and it's possible that somebody is in that house."

Benjamin nodded. "You watch my back, I'll watch yours."

"Then let's do it," Tom said and got back into his car. He turned and looked at Peyton, whose eyes radiated electric blue with anxiety.

"Promise me you won't move from the car until I come out to you."

"I promise," she said, her eyes shining earnestly. "Just hurry and tell me if she's in there or not."

With her promise ringing in his ear, Tom started the car and turned into the long driveway that led to the house.

It was a small home, and the deepening shadows of twilight couldn't hide the look of neglect that clung to the place. Still, lights spilled from the front window and a beat-up pickup was parked in the front.

Tom parked and cut the engine and without another word to Peyton got out of the car. As he approached the front door he hoped like hell he'd find inside the one thing that would erase the pain from Peyton's eyes.

Chapter 6

Peyton's heart was in her throat as she sat and stared at the house Tom and Benjamin had just disappeared inside of.

A young woman who had looked at Tom and Benjamin in surprise had opened the door. A thin young man had appeared at her side, then the two lawmen had gone into the house and Peyton hadn't been able to see anything else.

This whole thing felt wrong. What would that young couple have to do with a kidnapping, with a murder? They looked like teenagers. Why would they want to steal her baby?

She rubbed a hand across her forehead where a headache squeezed like a tight band. She leaned her head toward the open car window and drew in a deep breath of the warm night air.

She could hear nothing from the house. What was going on inside? Surely if Lilly were in there Tom would have already come out to get her.

Tom had said this was just the first of the tips to come in. Peyton had seen enough missing-children newscasts to realize that often in these cases thousands of tips came in from all over the country. The child was spotted in California or in Texas or in Florida, often all at the same time.

It could take weeks or even months to chase down all the leads this case might generate. Weeks and months that she wouldn't have sweet Lilly.

Hot tears burned her eyes as a well of grief threatened to consume her. The inner scream begged to be released, but she swallowed hard against it.

Lilly was at that stage of development where she changed almost every day. Peyton would be missing some of the most precious moments in her daughter's life.

She squeezed her eyelids closed and for the first time wondered if she would ever have Lilly back in her arms. How would she get through the rest of her life if they never found her baby?

How did Tom get up mornings without his little girl? How did any parent who had lost a child survive the grief?

She had to stay strong. She refused to break now. Right now all she knew was that Lilly was out there somewhere and hopefully would be found alive and well.

The minutes ticked by and twilight was replaced by the darkness of encroaching night. A glance at the clock let her know that Tom had only been in the house fifteen minutes, but if felt like hours had passed since he'd disappeared inside.

She felt as if in the space of seconds passing she'd transformed into a very old woman, with nothing but grief to keep her company.

The opening of the front door snapped her eyes back open and she looked toward the house to see Tom's silhouette as he approached the car.

He was halfway across the yard when she realized he was carrying something in his arms. Peyton froze and for a moment it felt as if her heart had stopped beating.

She heard the distinctive sound of a fussing baby, her baby. "Lilly?" The name whispered from her. She threw open the car door and sprang out, nearly tripping in the grass as she ran toward Tom.

"Lilly!" Tears half blurred her vision as she met him and he held out the infant.

Her baby! Oh, God, it was Lilly.

The deep sobs that Peyton had held in for so long ripped from her as she took Lilly from him and clutched the baby to her chest. She was laughing and crying at the same time as Tom grabbed her by the elbow and took her back to the car.

"I've got things to finish up inside. I'll be back in a

few minutes and we'll get the two of you home where you belong," Tom said. "I'll have a doctor come to check her out, but she seems okay."

She nodded absently, barely hearing him as she focused all her attention on her baby. Happy tears escaped her as Lilly smiled up at her.

The baby was wrapped in a pink blanket and Peyton quickly unwrapped her, needing to check her from head to toe to assure herself that Lilly was really okay.

She was clad in a pink T-shirt and a diaper and she smelled sweet and clean. It was obvious she'd been well taken care of, and for that Peyton was grateful.

At the moment Peyton didn't care how Lilly had come to be here and what the people inside the house had to do with India Richards. All she cared about was the baby in her arms, her beloved Lilly.

"Mommy missed you," she whispered as she held Lilly tight. She kissed her cheeks, her eyelids and forehead. She kissed Lilly's little toes as her heart sang. "Mommy missed you so very much." Lilly cuddled against her and within minutes had fallen asleep.

Peyton felt as if the world was suddenly right. Nothing mattered other than the fact that Lilly was safe and sound and back in her arms where she belonged.

Silent tears of joy fell as Peyton waited for Tom to come back to the car. What she wanted now was to get Lilly home.

It was nearly thirty minutes before Tom came back outside. He took Lilly from her arms and placed her in the car seat in the back, then got in behind the wheel and started the engine.

"Benjamin is going to stay here while I take you home. We're still in the process of taking statements from them. Their names are Benny and Molly Morris. They're nothing but a couple of kids playing house. Got married last year when they were eighteen years old."

"How did they get Lilly?" she asked.

"Apparently Molly is India's second cousin. India showed up here out of the blue on Tuesday afternoon with the baby. She told them that the baby belonged to a friend of hers who couldn't take care of her anymore and wanted to put her up for adoption. Molly has been trying to get pregnant for the last year without success, so India thought they might be interested in adopting. They took one look at Lilly and said they fell in love with her."

"They didn't question the legality of just being handed a baby?" Peyton asked incredulously.

He flashed her a quick glance. "Did I mention that they're really young? According to them, India was working with a lawyer and told them she'd be back with legal papers for them to sign."

"You think she just wanted to give them a baby? That's what this is all about?"

"I don't know yet," Tom replied. "According to the couple, they weren't close to India."

"Is there something physically wrong with them that they can't have a baby of their own?" she asked, trying to make sense of it.

"I asked them that and they both assured me that there was nothing wrong with them. But Molly had gotten impatient because it wasn't happening fast enough. She said the last time she'd talked to India she'd mentioned how frustrated she was about not getting pregnant."

"So she apparently went directly to their house right after she took Lilly," Peyton said thoughtfully. "And then went back to Black Rock and to that motel room? Why wouldn't she have run as far away and as fast as possible?"

"That's what I need to find out," he replied. He flashed her a quick smile. "At least this has a happy ending where you and Lilly are concerned."

Peyton's heart crunched a bit as she returned his smile. This must be a bittersweet moment for him, that he'd been able to return her child to her but had not been able to save his own little girl.

"Thank you, Tom. Thank you for everything you've done for me and for Lilly."

"Just doing my job," he replied lightly.

She felt his emotional distance and suddenly realized he was moving on. He'd achieved what he'd wanted in returning Lilly, and now it was time for him to get back to solving a murder and resuming his own life.

Even though she'd only known him a couple of days, she was surprised to realize she was going to miss him, that the intensity of emotions they had shared had forged a bond in her, but one that he obviously didn't feel.

He'd just been doing his job. When he'd held her as

she'd cried, it had been his duty as an officer of the law and nothing more.

Lilly slept the entire way home, and Tom and Peyton didn't speak for the remainder of the ride. It wasn't an uncomfortable silence but rather one of two people who were occupied with their own separate thoughts.

"What's going to happen to Benny and Molly?" she finally asked when he turned down the street where she lived.

"I don't know yet. It's too early to know if they'll be charged with anything." He pulled into her driveway and cut the engine. They both got out of the car and he opened the back door to get the sleeping Lilly from her seat.

As they walked up to the front porch he looked right carrying a baby in his arms, and Peyton's heart hurt for him as she thought of the child he had lost.

"I'll be in touch if I need anything from you, but Peyton, this isn't over yet. We still have a killer out there, and we don't know what his relationship might have been to you. You need to be careful, okay?" He transferred Lilly from his arms to hers. "I'll have a squad car stop in to check on you periodically."

"I don't know how to thank you enough," she said as tears once again burned at her eyes.

"You don't have to thank me. We got lucky, that's all," he replied.

She couldn't tell him that not only did she want to thank him for the return of her daughter but also for the fact that he'd instinctively known when she'd needed his strong arms around her. He'd known when to cover her cold, trembling hand with his own.

On impulse she reached up on her tiptoes with the intent of pressing her lips against his cheek. At the very last minute he dipped his head down and instead of his cheek her lips met his.

His mouth was softer, warmer than she'd anticipated, and what she'd meant as a simple thank-you kiss became so much more. Although his arms remained at his sides, a flicker of heat licked at her insides just before he stepped back from her.

His eyes were dark, impossible to read. "Good night, Peyton. I'll be in touch." Without another word he turned and left her porch.

She watched him go and felt a ridiculous stab in her heart as she realized he was for all intents and purposes out of her life.

She had her baby back and Tom had a killer to catch. There was no reason for their lives to intersect again in any real, meaningful way, and she wasn't sure why that thought made her incredibly sad.

The kiss was everything Tom had imagined it would be. Sweet, yet hot enough to flood his veins with heat. It had made him wonder what her skin would taste like beneath his lips, if she'd moan while he made love to her.

As he got into his car and left her house, he tried not to think about how soft and yielding her mouth had been against his, how much he'd wanted to deepen the kiss with his tongue.

Thank God they'd found the baby alive and well. Thank God there had been a happy ending for Peyton where the baby was concerned. In a million years he would never forget the look on Peyton's face when he'd returned Lilly to her. It had been such exquisite joy. He would love for her to experience that kind of joy every day for the rest of her life.

Unfortunately, the case wasn't wrapped up neat and tidy. One loose end was the fact that somebody had killed the kidnapper and Tom not only wanted to know who, but he also wanted to know why.

Cliff Gunther. The new name whirled around in his head. He needed to get Sam on finding out what he could about the waiter who had dated Peyton before her relationship with Tom. It was another loose end Tom didn't want to leave untended.

The next morning he was no closer to having answers than he'd been the night before. Not only did he have the weight of the India Richards case on his shoulders, but he was also wondering if Peyton was truly out of danger.

As he went into his office Sam greeted him with a frown. "Don't have much information for you on Cliff Gunther," he said.

Tom sat in the chair next to his desk. "What have you got?"

Sam pulled some papers in front of him. "Cliff Gunther, thirty-two years old. Born and raised in

Wichita and has a clean record except for a couple of speeding tickets. He quit his job two weeks ago and hasn't resurfaced anywhere else."

"Did you get an address?"

Sam nodded. "But one of his coworkers at the restaurant said he hasn't been at his apartment since he quit his job."

Tom frowned. "It could mean nothing, it could mean something. We need to dig a little deeper to find out where he is and what he's up to. If nothing else I need to exclude him in this case and move on to somebody else."

"Have you heard anything from Caleb?" Sam asked.

"Not yet. I'm hoping to hear something from him today about India Richards's life in Wichita. Meanwhile, I intend to spend the day trying to trace her movements while she was here in Black Rock."

"At least the baby is back where she belongs," Sam replied. "Peyton is probably having the best morning of her life this morning."

Tom nodded. He wished Sam hadn't said her name, hadn't put her back in his head. "I'll be in my office. Let me know when you have something more for me on Cliff Gunther."

"Will do," Sam agreed.

Tom went into his office and closed the door and tried to put Peyton Wilkerson out of his mind, with little success.

It felt strange not going directly to her house this

morning. In the span of just a couple of days, being with her had become a habit. But it was a habit he had to break.

Even though Peyton had been the first woman in a very long time to interest him on a male/female level, he could never be the man in her life.

He knew enough about her past, enough about her hopes and dreams to know that what she was looking for was a fantasy storybook ending. Tom was grounded in harsh reality too much to believe in those kinds of happily-ever-afters.

When he'd buried his precious Kelly he'd buried half his heart with her, and when Julie had walked away from him she'd taken the other half. There was nothing left for anyone else, and in any case he never wanted to be that vulnerable to the capricious nature of fate again. It was much safer, much easier to keep himself from ever caring too deeply about the people in his life.

He had to forget that kiss they'd shared, he had to stop thinking about Peyton as a sexy, loving woman and think of her only as a victim of a crime.

Besides, he had more important things on his mind, like the murder of India Richards. He also wanted to figure out who Peyton had had her run-in with at the grocery store. It might have nothing to do with what happened, but he wouldn't be satisfied until he checked out all leads.

Tom spent the morning chasing down information about India Richards. He knew there was no way she could have been in town for two months and not have met anyone but Peyton. Although the apartment where she'd been living had yielded few clues as to the life of the occupant, there had been some.

A discarded foam cup had held the name of a convenience store on the edge of town, and that was the first stop Tom made. Armed with a photo of India Richards, he entered the shop.

He recognized the older woman behind the counter and offered her a smile. "Hi, Margie."

"Morning, Tom. What brings you to this neck of the woods? I know it's not that sludge we call coffee."

Margie Meadows was a widow who lived in the house next to the Grayson ranch. At sixty-five years old she was as feisty as a woman half her age and had made it known that she was actively looking for a husband to replace the one she'd lost to a heart attack a year before.

"Or maybe you've finally come to your senses and decided what you need most in your life is a hot, sexy cougar like me," she added.

Tom laughed. "Ah, Margie, I have a feeling I could never keep up with you." He pulled the picture of India from his pocket. "I was wondering if you could tell me anything about this woman." He slid the picture across the counter to her.

"This is that woman who kidnapped that baby," she said. "Yeah, I've seen her in here a couple of times."

"Was she ever with anybody?"

Margie frowned. "Only once. I saw her get out of

Buck Harmon's truck and she came in and bought some beer then got back in his truck and they took off."

Buck Harmon. A burst of adrenaline shot through Tom. Buck was a twenty-four-year-old tough guy who lived fifteen miles outside of Black Rock and only ventured into town to frequent Harley's bar.

He was tall with sandy-colored hair and drove a black pickup. The only reason Tom hadn't thought of him before now was because he rarely saw Buck.

Was it merely a coincidence that Buck fit the description of the man who had cursed Peyton in the parking lot of the grocery store and had a connection to the woman who had kidnapped Lilly? Tom didn't believe in those kinds of coincidences.

He left the convenience store and headed out to Buck's place. Even with the little bit of information he now had, he couldn't make sense of the whole mess. He had the pieces of a puzzle but no puzzle box to look at to see how the pieces were supposed to fit together.

Buck lived in a small house that had belonged to his parents before they retired to Florida. He worked as a mechanic in the neighboring town of Little Creek and from what Tom knew had few friends. A phone call to the garage let Tom know that Buck didn't work on Saturdays, so Tom hoped to catch him at home.

Buck's pickup was in the driveway when Tom pulled up in front of the house, which looked as if it had been neglected for years. The paint was faded and peeling and a collection of old beer cans sat on top of the porch railing. The front yard was a graveyard of old tires and car parts.

As Tom approached the door he unfastened the snap of his holster, allowing for immediate access to his gun if it became necessary. He had no idea what role, if any, Buck might have played in either the kidnapping or the murder.

Buck answered Tom's knock. Clad in a T-shirt and a pair of boxers and with his hair disheveled as if he'd just climbed out of bed, he didn't looked pleased at the intrusion.

He narrowed his blue eyes and glared at Tom. "What's up? What are you doing here?"

"I need to ask you some questions, Buck. Can I come in?"

Buck raked a hand through his messy hair, then opened the screen door to allow Tom entry. "Excuse the mess," he said as he swept a pizza box and a newspaper off the shabby couch. "I don't usually get much company."

He threw his lanky body into the chair opposite the sofa. "So, what's going on?"

"I want to ask you about India Richards," Tom said.

"Who?" Buck frowned in incomprehension.

"You might have known her as Kathy Simon," Tom replied.

Buck's eyes narrowed once again. "Crazy chick. I met her one night at Harley's, and we kicked it together for a couple of hours. I didn't have anything to do with whatever trouble she got herself into, and I sure as hell didn't kill her."

"What can you tell me about her?" Tom asked. He wasn't sure if he could believe a word that came out of Buck's mouth, but for the moment he was willing to listen to whatever he had to say.

"Not much. She liked to dance, liked to drink and I thought she was going to like other things, too, if you get my drift. But she told me she had a boyfriend and wasn't going to cheat on him."

"Did she say anything else about this boyfriend of hers?"

"Not really. I got the feeling he might be married."

"Did she tell you that?" Tom asked.

Buck shook his head. "Nah, it was just the impression I got, that she was just hanging out here in Black Rock until he could be with her."

"Did she say if he was from Black Rock?"

"Not specifically, but I assumed he was."

Back and forth it went as Tom continued to question him. By the time Tom left just before noon, he didn't have any definitive answers, but he had more directions to explore in his investigation.

Buck had told him that on the night of India's murder he was in Harley's back room playing pool. Tom knew it was going to be difficult to check the alibi. The crowd that hung at Harley's could be a tough one, and few of them would be willing to answer questions.

Tom was in his car and headed back to his office when his cell phone rang. It was Caleb telling Tom that he was back from Wichita. The two agreed to meet for lunch at the local café.

It was just before noon when Tom parked in front of the Black Rock Café. He'd skipped breakfast and his stomach rumbled with hunger. The food at the café was the best in town.

Harry Thompson, the owner, greeted Tom as he walked through the door. Harry was a walking advertisement for the quality of the food he offered. Heavyset and with a broad cheerful smile, he looked like a man who knew how to enjoy a good meal.

"Your brother is waiting for you in a booth in the back," Harry said. "And the chicken fried steak is exceptional today."

"Thanks, Harry. Sounds good." Tom made his way through the tables to the booth where Caleb waited for him. As he sat, the waitress appeared and they placed their orders.

Tom relayed to Caleb what he'd found out from Buck, and by that time their lunches had arrived. "So, what did you find out in Wichita?" he asked.

"First of all, Rick Powell has a great reputation in town. Tough on crime, a stand-up guy. Nobody I spoke to had a bad word to say about him. He's definitely ambitious. According to his coworkers, he has an eye on the D.A. position and eventually wants to get into the national politic scene. On the other hand, India Richards didn't have that kind of a reputation."

Caleb paused to cut into his chicken fried steak. He took a bite then washed it down with his soda and continued. "I contacted a friend of hers. Her name is Brandy Wine—no joke, that's her real name. Anyway, she told me India ran with a rough crowd, that she always figured she'd wind up either dead or in prison."

"Did she say what brought India to Black Rock?" Tom asked.

"A man, although Brandy didn't have a name."

Tom frowned. "Buck said basically the same thing. He also thought the man might be married."

"Maybe India mistook an affair for something more important. Maybe she was pressing Mr. Married to come clean to his wife and he wasn't prepared to do that," Caleb said.

"Then it's possible her murder had nothing to do with Lilly's kidnapping." Tom leaned back in his seat and released a deep sigh. "It seems like the more information we learn, the more complicated things become."

He looked up and froze at the sight of Peyton coming in the door. He'd spent the morning trying his damnedest not to think about her, and there she was, bigger than life, beelining toward him with Lilly in her arms and a wide, joyful smile on her face.

The sight of her reminded him of the kiss they had shared and a small flame ignited in the pit of his stomach.

As she reached their booth she nodded to Caleb, then turned to Tom. "Hi. We were just on our way to your office when I saw your car parked outside."

She looked gorgeous in a pale pink sundress that

bared her creamy, slender shoulders and emphasized her cool blond coloring.

"What's up?" he asked, trying to maintain his professional composure.

"Lilly and I would like to invite you to dinner tomorrow night as a thank-you," she said.

"That's not necessary," he protested.

"Don't be silly, brother," Caleb said. "When a pretty lady invites you to dinner you should always accept."

"Tom, please. I'd really like to do this for you," she said.

Thanks to Caleb, Tom felt as if there was no way to decline the offer without looking like a jerk. "What time?" he asked, deciding it was easier to give in that to make a big deal out of it. After all, it was just a meal.

Her eyes lit with pleasure. "Shall we say around six-thirty?"

"All right," he agreed.

"Wonderful. And, Tom, be sure to come hungry." With the smile still on her face, she murmured a goodbye and walked away.

Tom watched the sway of her hips as she left. *Come hungry.* What she didn't realize was that she stirred a hunger inside him, a hunger that shouldn't be sated.

"I think you might need this," Caleb said as he pulled out his wallet and withdrew a condom package. He laid it on the table between them.

"Jeez, Caleb, put that away," Tom exclaimed.

Caleb grinned. "If you want it put away you'd better put it in your wallet."

Tom snatched it up and shoved it into his pocket. "I don't know why you think I'll need it. She invited me for dinner, that's all."

Caleb leaned back in the booth with a grin. "I might not know everything there is to know about investigating crimes, but one thing I know is women, and brother, that woman has the hots for you."

"That's ridiculous," Tom scoffed. "You heard what she said. She just wants to thank me."

Caleb leaned forward, the smile on his face fading away. "Why don't you allow yourself to enjoy whatever it is she's offering? Haven't you punished yourself enough for the past?"

Tom stiffened. "I'm not punishing myself for anything—this subject is now officially closed." He picked up his fork to finish his lunch. At this moment he wasn't sure what was going to be more difficult, solving India Richards's murder or getting through tomorrow night's dinner with Peyton without doing something stupid.

Chapter 7

The house was spotless and the scent of chicken and freshly baked rolls filled the air. Peyton felt ridiculously nervous as she poured herself a glass of wine and sat at the table adorned with her good dishes and silverware. Lilly was in her infant swing nearby, cooing with happiness as she swung to and fro.

This was supposed to be a simple thank-you meal, but for Peyton it was much more. With the trauma of Lilly's kidnapping behind her, over the past day she'd been able to think of nothing but Tom.

Without the fear for Lilly that had gripped her heart, it was now open to all the feelings she'd suppressed where the handsome lawman was concerned.

She liked him. She liked him a lot. Her feelings for him had little to do with the fact that he'd successfully gotten her baby back into her arms. It was so much more than that.

His quiet confidence was so different than Rick's bravado, and yet she felt so much more comfortable in Tom's company. His quiet, steady ways soothed her, but at the same time his sexy brown eyes sparked a flame of excitement in her that she wanted to explore.

She'd thought she'd seen a flicker of desire in his eyes, especially in those moments just after they'd kissed. The truth was she wanted Tom Grayson. She wasn't a fool enough to believe herself in love with him, not after knowing him only a couple of days, but she wanted to get to know him better, and that's what tonight was all about.

Even though she was excited to spend time with him, the nerves that fluttered through her as she waited his arrival surprised her.

A glance at the clock let her know he was due to arrive within minutes. She had a feeling Tom was a man who would rarely be late.

Rick had rarely been on time for anything. There had always been one last phone call he needed to make, one more e-mail to send before he could give her his attention.

At precisely six-thirty her doorbell rang. She downed the last of her wine, ran quick fingers through her hair and then hurried to the door to greet him.

As she opened the door, her heart swelled at the sight of him. It was the first time she'd seen him out of uniform. He looked amazingly masculine and hot in a pair of jeans and a blue striped short-sleeved dress shirt.

"Tom, I'm so glad you came," she said as she opened the door to allow him inside.

"Thanks for inviting me," he replied. He looked ill at ease as he stepped into the living room. He held out a bottle of wine. "I didn't know if I should bring white or red, so I guessed at white."

"It's chicken, so that's perfect," she replied and took the bottle from him. "In fact, I have to confess, I've already had a glass of wine. Come on in and I'll pour you a glass so you can catch up."

She was acutely conscious of him just behind her as she led him into the kitchen. She could smell the familiar scent of him, that spicy cologne that somehow smelled like a combination of sweet comfort and heady desire.

As Tom walked into the kitchen his lips curved into a smile as he saw Lilly. "It's nice to know she's where she belongs," he said as Peyton gestured him into a chair at the table.

"You have no idea," Peyton replied as she poured him a glass of wine and handed it to him. "The night I got her home I could barely let her go so she could sleep in her crib." A new burst of emotion welled up in Peyton's chest as she thought of how close she'd come to losing Lilly forever.

She shoved those terrible thoughts aside. Tonight was the time to be happy, to celebrate that Lilly was home and Tom was here.

"Dinner should be ready in about fifteen minutes," she said as she poured herself another glass of wine. "I hope you like chicken cordon bleu."

One of his dark brows lifted. "I do, but that's a lot of work."

"Cooking has become a hobby of mine," she said as she leaned against the counter. "When I was seventeen I got a job in an upscale restaurant and the chef became a mentor of sorts. In our slow time he would teach me cooking techniques."

"So why teaching? Why didn't you become a chef?" he asked.

She could tell by his posture that he was beginning to relax. She wanted him relaxed. She wanted him to enjoy dinner with her.

"I love kids. I always wanted to be a teacher. The other jobs I had were just the means to get me money to pay for my college education. What about you? Did you always want to be a sheriff?"

He leaned back in the chair and his eyes held the warmth of memories. "When I was eighteen years old I was flirting with the other side of the law," he admitted. "I thought I was a tough guy and was always ready for a brawl. The sheriff at the time was a close friend of my father's, and my dad arranged for me to work with him part-time on the weekends. It was the best thing my dad ever did for me. When I was twenty-one I became a full-time deputy, and when I was twenty-eight I became sheriff."

"And what a wonderful role model you've become for your siblings," she said.

"Yeah, law enforcement in Black Rock has definitely become a family affair." He finished his wine, and Peyton began to put the meal on the table.

"Is there anything I can do to help?" he asked.

"Absolutely not," she replied. "You just sit there and relax."

It took her only minutes to get everything on the table and join him there. As they ate, Lilly smiled and babbled, perfectly satisfied in her swing and with her mother in sight.

The conversation continued to flow throughout the meal. She was delighted by the stories Tom told of growing up with his brothers and sister. His obvious commitment to and love of his family only made him more appealing.

She shared with him the loneliness she'd felt as a child, growing up virtually alone in a world of adults behaving badly. "I remember one particular night when we were homeless and my mother left me alone in the car. It was in a scary part of town where the only people on the streets were thugs and prostitutes. I hid in the backseat beneath on old blanket and prayed that I'd still be alive in the morning."

Tom gazed at her, his eyes dark and filled with concern. "How old were you?"

"Nine. That night I swore to myself I'd have something better when I grew up, that I wouldn't make the same choices my mother made and that my husband and any children I had would be the most important things in my life." She grinned. "I managed to get it all a little bit backward and got the child before I got the man."

By that time they had finished eating and Tom insisted he help her clear the table. Instantly the kitchen seemed to shrink as he filled it with his presence. By the time they'd finished clearing things from the table, Lilly had fallen asleep in the swing.

"How about some coffee?" she suggested as she put the last plate in the dishwasher.

"Sounds good," he agreed.

"Why don't you make yourself comfortable in the living room and I'll put the coffee on and put Lilly to bed."

"Why don't you take care of Lilly and I'll make the coffee?" he suggested.

She nodded. "Sounds like a plan." She scooped the sleeping baby up and left the kitchen.

As she walked down the hallway holding Lilly she thought of the man in her kitchen. Throughout the meal she'd been intensely aware of him, the memory of the kiss they'd shared replaying over and over in her head.

The hunger she felt for him was like nothing she'd felt for Rick. This was stronger, more intense, and she wondered if it was because of the kidnapping, because of India's murder.

She was struck with a feeling of how important it was to grasp every moment of life, to reach for what you wanted because life was too short. She wasn't in love with Tom, but she was in serious lust, and right now that felt like enough.

Gently she placed Lilly in her crib, kissed her on her sweet cheek and left the room. She had no idea what to expect for the rest of the evening, but she was eager to see how the night would unfold.

The minute Peyton carried Lilly out of the kitchen, Tom set about making the coffee and mentally cursed his younger brother. The condom Caleb had given him burned in his back pocket, but it didn't burn as hot as the desire he'd fought all through the meal.

The burn had begun the moment she'd opened the door. Dressed in a blue sundress that perfectly matched her eyes, and with her hair pulled back at her nape exposing dainty ears and the lovely length of her slender neck, she'd taken his breath away.

There was something about her that broke his heart just a little bit. Maybe it was because he could so easily imagine her as that small, frightened girl struggling to survive in a world where she didn't belong.

But it wasn't sympathy for what she'd gone through that boiled the blood in his veins, that made him think about running his mouth down the length of her neck.

It was the evocative scent of her, the press of her breasts against the blue material and the slender, curvy bare legs beneath her dress that had him half dizzy with desire.

It would be absolutely wrong to make a move on her. He knew what she wanted most in her life, and Tom wasn't and could never be that man. She wanted a man who would love her, and Tom had no love to give. But that didn't mean he had no desire to give.

He was pouring the coffee when she returned to the kitchen. "She's a good baby," he said as they carried their cups into the living room and sat side-by-side on the sofa.

"She's a great baby," Peyton replied. "She rarely fusses and has been sleeping through the night for a while now."

"Has Rick been back to see her since she got home?"

Peyton nodded. "He drove in yesterday morning and spent a couple of hours playing with her."

"Any chance you two will get back together?" He half hoped she'd say yes. Rick seemed like a stand-up guy, and that would put an end to what Tom felt, where she was concerned.

She laughed. "No way. Neither of us have any desire to get back together. Rick will probably always be in my life, but only as the man who is Lilly's father."

"I found the man who had that altercation in the parking lot with you," he said. Maybe he wouldn't notice the heat radiating from her and the heady scent of her perfume if he talked about work.

"It wasn't a real altercation," she countered. "But who is he?"

"His name is Buck Harmon. He lives in a neighboring small town, and he knew India."

Her eyes widened. "Did he have something to do with the kidnapping? With India's murder?"

"I don't know yet. According to what he told me, he met India at Harley's bar and they hung out together for a night. He says he had no idea that she was going to kidnap a baby, and he sure doesn't know who murdered her, but I'm checking him out."

"It's a mess, isn't it?"

"Yeah, it is. To make matters more complicated, Buck had the impression that India had a lover here in town, a married lover. Caleb got the same information from a friend of India's in Wichita."

Peyton frowned thoughtfully. "So maybe the lover couldn't have children and wanted them, so he and India cooked up the scheme to take Lilly, then run away and live together like a family."

"Maybe, although there's also the possibility that the married man didn't expect his lover to show up here in Black Rock. Maybe he murdered India to save his marriage."

"That's a lot of maybes," she said.

"And that's all we've got right now," he replied with a touch of frustration.

She smiled at him and placed her hand on his forearm. "You'll figure it out, Tom. I have all the confidence in the world that you'll solve this mess."

He would have been so much better if she hadn't touched him, but the feel of her warm hand on his skin reminded him of how soft her lips had been beneath his, how warm and sexy she'd felt in his arms.

It had been so long since he'd been with a woman, so long since he'd even allowed himself the pleasure of feminine company. But there was something about Peyton Wilkerson that moved him both on an emotional and a physical level.

"I should probably go," he finally said. This woman felt dangerous to him, to his sense of peace.

"So early? I still have a cherry chocolate cake for dessert. Surely you'll at least stay for dessert." She looked at him wistfully.

"Since you went to all that trouble, I suppose I could stay for a piece of cake," he replied.

"Great! I'll just go get it."

As she left the sofa and went into the kitchen, Tom released a deep sigh. This was all Caleb's fault. If he hadn't given Tom that condom then Tom wouldn't have sex on his mind. And if Peyton didn't look so sexy and hot, he wouldn't have sex with her on his mind.

She came back into the living room carrying a tray with two dessert plates with cake, forks and napkins. She set the tray in the center of the coffee table and then handed him one of the pieces of cake.

"This looks sinful," he said, eyeing the dark chocolate with bits of cherries, but he was thinking about the curve of her breasts that were visible just above the deep neckline of her dress.

"My philosophy is that if it looks good, feels good or tastes good it can't be all wrong." She picked up her plate and fork.

Her words did nothing to dispel Tom's wayward

thoughts. He felt like an awkward teenager pumped with hormones and on a date with the school beauty queen.

"When do you start work at the school?" he asked.

"Two weeks." She frowned and looked down at the cake. "I have to confess I'm not sure what I'm going to do. I'm just not ready to leave Lilly with anyone, and I can't exactly take her to school with me."

"Where do you plan to take her?"

"Portia's Playpen."

"She'll be fine there," Tom assured her. "Portia Perez is devoted to the kids in her day care."

"She just seemed young," Peyton replied.

Tom smiled. "She's twenty-seven and has a degree in early childhood development."

"How do you know so much about her?" She slid a forkful of the cake into her mouth and then licked the side of her upper lip.

Tom stared down at his own piece of dessert as a new fire of desire crashed through him. "Portia and Caleb dated when they were in high school. They broke up when Portia went to college. Portia has a great reputation, and lots of mothers here in town trust her with their children."

"That makes me feel better. One of my goals over the next two weeks is to get out and meet some of the people here." She set her plate back on the coffee table and leaned back against the sofa cushion.

"One of the things I realized during the ordeal with Lilly is that I haven't made any friends here. I was isolated with just India hanging around. I don't even know my neighbors," she said with a frown.

"To the left are Jane and Harvey Carter. You probably haven't met them yet. They're retired and spend most of the summers at their son's place in Maine. On the right are the Burkes, Carrie and Mike."

He began to relax again as he told her about some of the people in her neighborhood, and it wasn't long before he was describing some of the more colorful characters in town.

He loved the sound of her laughter and found himself exaggerating quirks of the people in order to hear her deep-throated laugh.

His laughter halted abruptly when she reached out and ran her finger across the side of his upper lip. "You had a little frosting there," she said.

He reached for his napkin, his breath caught painfully in his chest. But before he could wipe his mouth, she leaned toward him, and he knew by the look on her face that she wanted—needed—to be kissed. And God help him, he complied.

He leaned forward and captured her mouth with his. In an instant she was in his arms, her mouth open to him. She tasted of sweet, dark chocolate and hot desire, and as her tongue met his he was momentarily lost in the simple pleasure of kissing her.

One minute they were kissing still seated side by side and the next moment she was on her back beneath him on the sofa.

Their tongues battled in a hunger that sprang up

instantly. Her arms wound around his back, and her fingers played in the hair at the nape of his neck, creating a sizzling electricity that stung through him.

He wanted her with a raging need and tasted her desire for him on her lips. It had been so long, so aching long since he'd lost himself in a woman, and as they continued to kiss he realized how easy it would be for him to lose himself in Peyton.

Still, someplace in the back of his mind he knew this was wrong, that he was absolutely the wrong man to be kissing her, to be feeling the warmth of her body beneath him.

Reluctantly he broke the kiss and sat up. "Peyton, we can't do this," he said even as he felt his arousal tight against his jeans.

"Why not?" Her voice was low and sexy as she sat up and gazed at him.

He couldn't look at her, not with her mouth moist and red from his kisses, not with her eyes so deep blue with desire. He got up from the sofa, needing to distance himself from her.

"Peyton, I'm not the man you're looking for in your life."

She got up from the sofa and smiled at him. "I'm just looking for tonight, Tom, not tomorrow or the day after. I want you, and I can tell that you want me, too."

His breath caught in his throat as she moved to stand in front of him, so close he could feel her warm breath on his neck, so close her breasts touched his chest. "We're not foolish kids, Tom. We're both adults, and I can't think of a single reason why we can't make love tonight."

Tom tried to think of all the reasons it would be a bad idea, but he couldn't think as she wound her arms around his neck and pressed herself intimately against him.

"I'm not the man you want," he finally managed to say.

"You're the man I want right now," she replied. "And that's enough for me."

Brain dead. He was completely and totally brain dead. She'd effectively removed every concern he had, and his desire to take her was suddenly far stronger than anything else.

She must have seen his answer in his eyes, for she took him by the hand and led him down the hallway to her bedroom.

His last rational thought was a mental thank-you to Caleb, who had made sure he was prepared for a simple dinner of thanks with Peyton.

Chapter 8

Peyton's heart beat wildly as they entered her bedroom. She'd told Tom the truth: at that moment, she wasn't thinking of the future. She only knew her need for him now.

It was crazy after knowing him such a short period of time, but she already felt intimately involved with him. What she wanted was to be naked in his arms, to feel his heart beating against her own as they made love.

The minute they were in the bedroom he claimed her mouth again, kissing her with such searing intent that her bones seemed to melt in her body.

As his mouth left hers and trailed down her neck, she began to unfasten the buttons on his shirt. With several of the buttons undone, she slid her arms around his warm, bare chest, and at the same time he unzipped the zipper that ran up the back of her dress.

He shoved it off her shoulders and it fell to the floor, leaving her clad only in a lacy bra and matching panties. "Just let me look at you," he whispered as she stepped back from him.

In the illumination from the bedside lamp, his eyes glowed like a wild animal's as he visually devoured her. She felt his gaze like pinpricks of heat lingering on the fullness of her breasts, lowering to her hips and legs.

"God, you're beautiful," he said as he pulled off his shirt.

"So are you," she replied as she gazed at his sharply cut, muscular chest. Before her legs could turn completely weak, she pulled down the bedspread and slid beneath the sheets.

"Peyton, are you sure this is what you want to do?" He shifted from one foot to the other. "I don't want this to be about gratitude."

She laughed. "Tom, I'm grateful for the guy who throws my newspaper on my porch in the mornings, but you don't see him in my bed. This isn't about giving you something, it's about giving myself something. I want you, and nothing is going to change my mind."

Her words snapped his inertia and her heart beat even faster as he placed his wallet on the nightstand and took off his pants.

"I'm glad it's not the newspaper man in your bed," he said as he slid beneath the sheets next to her and gathered her into his arms.

She smiled at him. "Me, too."

He captured her smile with his mouth, and there was no more time for levity. As he kissed her he reached around behind her and unfastened her bra and then covered her breasts with his warm palms.

She closed her eyes against the sensations that coursed through her, and as he moved down her body she wrapped her fingers in his thick, dark hair. A moan escaped her as he captured one of her nipples in his mouth.

His skin was hot against hers, and she loved the feel of it. She could feel the length of his hardness pressed against her thigh, and knowing she had caused his arousal only increased the sexual excitement that winged through her.

He kissed and nibbled and licked first one turgid nipple and then the other and she reached down and stroked the length of him through his cotton boxers.

He gasped and slid his hands beneath her buttocks to pull down her panties. She aided him, raising her hips to allow him to take the wisp of silk from her. When she was completely naked he took off his boxers and then pulled her back to him.

Her skin sizzled against his, and as he cupped her face with his hands and kissed her again she felt the absolute rightness of being with him.

Even though her entire body sang with sexual want, she'd never felt so safe in a man's arms. Although Tom caressed her with hunger and passion, beneath it was a tenderness that was as exciting and wonderful as anything.

As his hands slid down the length of her, over the rise of her breasts and down the flat of her stomach, her breath caught in the back of her throat as he touched her inner thigh with his hot fingers.

"Peyton," he whispered, his voice deeper than usual. "It's been a long time since I've been with anyone."

"And you make me feel as if this is the very first time for me," she replied.

He gazed down at her. "Then that's all the more reason it should be slow and sweet, but I don't think I have slow in me right now."

She smiled and placed her hand on the side of his face. "Just love me, Tom. Short and sweet or fast and frantic, I just want you to make love to me."

His mouth crashed down to hers, and at the same time his hand moved from her thigh to the very center of her. A deep moan built up inside her as his intimate touch shot sweet sensations through her.

He knew exactly where to touch, precisely how much pressure to use to bring her to the brink of climax. As he took her over the edge, she stiffened and cried out his name as wave after wave of pleasure crashed over her.

Before she could catch her breath he rolled over and grabbed his pants and pulled out a condom package. He ripped it open and put it on, then with his breath hitching in his throat he moved on top of her.

She welcomed him, opening her legs and grabbing

his shoulders. He moved into her and froze, his eyes narrowing as he gazed down at her. "Peyton, you feel so good." He lowered his head and kissed her with a tenderness that nearly brought tears to her eyes.

As the kiss ended he began to move against her, into her. Slowly at first, he stroked deep and easy, and she arched up to meet his every thrust. But it didn't take long for their movements to become faster and more frantic.

Peyton was lost in him, in the heat of his body and the arms that held her. She was lost to the fiery pleasure that he gave her as he thrust again and again.

A building tension welled up inside her and she knew he was reaching the end. His body shook with faint tremors and his grunts of pleasure brought her closer to her own climax.

As it rushed over her and she cried out his name, he stiffened against her and collapsed with his chest just to her side.

For several long moments neither of them spoke as they waited for breathing to return to normal and speech to become possible once again.

"Wow," he finally said.

Peyton giggled. "My sentiments exactly."

He stroked a finger down the side of her face. "You are amazing."

She smiled. "I never believe the praise of a naked man in my bed after lovemaking."

He laughed. "It's more dangerous to believe the words of a naked man in your bed *before* lovemaking."

She laughed again. "I never thought of that." Reluctantly she disengaged from him. "I need to go check on Lilly," she said. She leaned over and kissed him on the cheek. "I'll be right back."

She slid out of bed and grabbed the robe that hung on a hook just inside her closet. Wrapping herself up in the cool cotton, she left the room.

Her entire body tingled with residual heat from Tom. He'd been everything she'd wanted him to be—sexy yet tender, commanding but gentle.

It hadn't just been the physical aspect of what they'd shared that warmed her. Emotionally it felt right to be with Tom. He fit into her world like no man had before.

As she walked into the nursery, a smile curved her lips at the sight of Lilly sleeping soundly in the crib. There was a peace in her heart she hadn't felt for a long time.

She covered Lilly with a sheet and stifled the impulse to lean down and kiss her little cheek. She didn't want to awaken her.

When Peyton returned to the bedroom she was disappointed to see Tom up and with his pants on. "Oh, you're leaving? I was hoping that maybe you'd spend the night."

He reached for his shirt and shook his head. He didn't look at her as he pulled on his shirt and buttoned it up. "I've got to go. I've still got things to do tonight."

She could taste the regret in the air, coming off him in waves. He grabbed his wallet from the nightstand

and shoved it into his back pocket, then finally met her gaze.

"Peyton, I loved making love with you, but it's not going to happen again." He shoved his hands in his pockets, a gesture she recognized as defensiveness. "You deserve to find the man of your dreams, and I can't be that man."

"And I think maybe you're selling yourself short," she replied, but there was no way she was going to argue with him, to try to make him see that they had something special and should explore where it took them.

Instead she walked silently behind him as he left her room and headed for the front door. When he reached the door, he turned back to face her. "Thank you, Peyton, for being an amazingly strong, loving woman. You're going to make a wonderful wife for some lucky man."

He drew in a deep, visible breath. "And all that talk about you getting out and meeting people. I need to remind you that we don't know if the danger to you has passed. Until we know who was working with India and what connection they might have to you—to Lilly—the threat isn't gone. I don't want you leaving this house unless I or one of my deputies are with you. Make sure your door is locked at all times. I don't want to scare you, but until we have India's murderer behind bars, there's still danger."

He didn't wait for her response but turned and walked out the front door. She stood and watched as he got into his car.

She felt as if something had ended before it had really

begun, and what surprised her more than anything was the sadness that filled her heart. And as she thought of his final words, she quickly closed and locked her door as a new burst of fear rushed through her.

Tom didn't go home. He was too restless, too filled with alien emotions to try to sleep. Instead he drove north, toward the family ranch. He needed some time to process what had just happened, time so that the scent of Peyton would wear off his skin. A visit to Jacob was just what he needed. It had been too long since he'd spoken with him.

In another lifetime, under different circumstances, he might have found himself falling in love with Peyton. She was bright and brave, sexy and funny—she possessed all the qualities he liked in a woman.

But she was too late.

And he wasn't the man she thought he was.

As always when he turned down the lane that led to the Grayson ranch, a sense of homecoming filled him. The house where he'd grown up was once a three-bedroom ranch, but as the kids had come, additions had been added so that now it boasted four bedrooms, three baths and a huge family room addition on the back.

It was a working cattle ranch with acres of pasture and a large barn to house the horses they all owned. As he drove past the house and the barn he thought of his childhood.

It had been a happy one. Sure, there had been chaos and noise much of the time, but there had also been plenty of love and security, two necessities that Peyton hadn't known in her childhood.

A narrow dirt road took him past a large pond and to a grove of trees where a small cottage was visible amid the large, lush trees.

This house and the surrounding land had once belonged to a neighbor, but big Jim Grayson had bought him out. Through the years this little cottage had served many uses—a guesthouse for visiting relatives, a romantic getaway for the harried parents of five kids, and as home for one or the other of those kids as they became adults.

Even though it felt late as Tom pulled up in front of the cottage, a glance at the clock let him know it was just after ten. A single light burned in the front window, letting him know that Jacob was still awake.

Of all his brothers, Tom had always been closest to Jacob. It had just worked out that the two eldest were close, and Caleb and Benjamin were close, and they had all spoiled Brittany rotten.

A surge of irritation filled him as he thought of his wayward sister. This wasn't the first time she'd just up and disappeared. Six months earlier she'd gone to Las Vegas to marry a man she'd only known for three months. Thankfully, she'd come to her senses before the wedding could take place, but she'd hidden out for two weeks rather than face her brothers.

But what weighed on his heart more than anything at the moment was the fact that he'd made love to Peyton when he'd known deep in his soul that it was the wrong thing to do. Worse than that, he wanted to do it again.

He knocked once and heard his brother yell for him to come in. He walked in to see Jacob in the recliner in the small living room. As always, the sight of Jacob sent a small shock through Tom.

His black hair had become long and shaggy, emphasizing the lean angles of his face. His jaw held the growth of several days of whiskers, giving him the aura of a man who didn't care.

"Grab a beer if you want," Jacob said as he lifted a bottle of his own to his lips.

Tom went into the kitchen and grabbed a beer from the fridge, then returned to the living room and sank down on the sofa.

"Heard you've had a tough week," Jacob said.

"Yeah, it's been rough," Tom agreed. "Did Benjamin fill you in?"

"Yeah. Missing baby, pretty single mother, a murdered woman and our missing sister. I think Benjamin has told me everything except what he had to eat for lunch on Tuesday," Jacob said dryly.

"If you'd get out of that chair and out of this cabin, Benjamin wouldn't have to keep updating you with what's going on in town and with the family," Tom replied.

Jacob said nothing but instead tipped his bottle to his lips and took a deep drink. He'd been doing that a lot lately. He'd come home thin, his eyes shadowed with secrets he refused to share with anyone. But Tom knew that Jacob wouldn't talk about what had put the darkness in his eyes until he was good and ready.

For the next few minutes the two talked about the kidnapping and murder. "Likely suspects?" Jacob asked.

"That's the problem. There aren't many. Buck Harmon spent some time with India but insists he was playing pool in the back room at Harley's when she was murdered. Johnny Boyd confirmed it, but those two are thick as thieves, so who knows if it's the truth or not. Caleb is checking out some of the people from India's past, and Peyton came up with the name of an old boyfriend, but it looks like this murder isn't going to be an easy solve."

"Some of them never get solved," Jacob said darkly. He finished his beer and set the bottle on the table next to his chair. "So tell me about the woman."

"What woman?" Tom asked.

"Benjamin told me he thought there was something going on between you and the mother of the baby."

Tom frowned. Although this was what he'd come to talk about, he found himself reluctant now to discuss his crazy feelings for Peyton.

"She's an amazing woman, strong and bright and sexy. But, I have no interest in pursuing anything with her."

"You haven't had any interest in pursuing anyone since Julie left you," Jacob observed.

"I tried it once, and I have no intention of trying it again," Tom replied.

"You're in a box of your own making, Tom. You've convinced yourself that you failed, and that's not reality. If anyone should try it again, it should be you."

"That's funny coming from a guy who's locked himself inside this house and refuses to leave, doesn't even want anyone to know he's here."

"I have my reasons."

"You sure you don't want to talk about them?" Tom asked.

"Positive." There was a definite edge to Jacob's voice that warned Tom from pushing. "You know, someday you might want to let yourself talk about Julie and Kelly. You never really gave yourself any time to grieve."

"That's ridiculous, of course I grieved. Besides, there's nothing to talk about. Kelly died, Julie left and that's the end of the story," Tom replied.

For the next hour the two talked about safe subjects— the hot weather, the ranch and the new veterinarian who had set up practice in town.

"He was out here the other day to look at one of the horses who got into some brambles," Jacob said. "Benjamin seemed impressed with him."

"I haven't met him yet," Tom said.

"I'm surprised. From what Benjamin said, he and his wife and family have been in town a couple of months now."

"A couple of months? I didn't realize it had been that long. Maybe it's time I had a visit with the new vet in town. Did Benjamin mention where they're from?"

"No. Why? You've got that sheriff look in your eyes," Jacob said.

Tom shrugged. "Just a thought. One of our theories is that India came here to be close to a married lover. She moved here two months ago, and from what you've just told me, it might have been around the same time that the new vet showed up here in town."

"Sounds like you're grasping at straws," Jacob observed.

"I am," Tom admitted, "but at the moment straws are all I have left." He released a weary sigh. "Not only do I have a murder to solve, but I don't know if Peyton is out of danger yet. Until I find out who killed India, I won't know what the connection is with Peyton, and that worries me."

Jacob raked a hand through his thick, unruly hair and gave Tom a half grin. "Then I guess it's your job to make sure she stays safe."

"I guess so," Tom agreed.

Minutes later, when he was back in his car and headed home, he wondered how in the hell he was going to keep Peyton safe *and* keep his distance.

Chapter 9

It had been three days since Tom had come to dinner, three days since they had made love, and Peyton realized he had no intention of sharing any relationship with her other than a professional one.

He'd called several times each day asking if she needed anything, reminding her that he didn't think it was a good idea for her to go out and about, but he'd been cool and distant each time.

She couldn't help but be disappointed. Despite everything, she'd hoped for more.

Still, she tried not to sit around and mope, even though her heart had been bruised a little. Monday she cleaned the house from top to bottom and played with Lilly.

Although she tried not to think about Tom, thoughts

of him refused to leave her head. She'd thought he cared about her, beyond their roles of sheriff and victim. It had been in his touch when he held her hand, it had been in his eyes when he'd looked at her. There had been something there, something strictly male and female that had nothing to do with their roles in the drama.

Still, she couldn't make him acknowledge it or embrace it. He'd wished her well and sent her on her way—alone, as she'd been for most of her life.

Tuesday was a longer day. With little to do, she wandered the house and finally sat at the kitchen table and made lessons plans for the fall.

Today, Wednesday, had been the longest day of all. Cabin fever hit hard. How long could she stay cooped up in the house worried about some threat that might or might not exist? How long was she willing to keep her life on hold?

By evening she'd decided she wasn't willing to put off her life any longer. She wanted to get out of the house. She wanted to go to the park and breathe in some fresh air, sit and maybe visit with whoever might also be there.

With India's death, some of the fear for Lilly's safety had vanished. She believed Tom's theory, that India had moved to Black Rock to be near a lover. Peyton thought it was possible that India had stolen Lilly in the deluded belief that she'd present her lover with a ready-made family. Once she'd actually taken Lilly she must have panicked and instead of keeping her had taken her to her cousin's house.

Crazy love, that's what India had apparently felt for her lover. And Peyton believed it was that crazy love that had gotten her killed.

But Peyton couldn't remain locked up in her house until her killer was caught. What if the killer was never caught? At some point she had to start living again.

It was just after seven when Peyton called Tom. "I'm sorry to bother you," she said when he answered. "But I just wanted to let you know that I'm taking Lilly to the park for a little while. It's a beautiful evening, and if I have to stay in this house another minute I think I'll scream."

There was a moment of silence. "I'll meet you there," he finally said.

"Oh, Tom, I don't want you to have to babysit me," she protested.

"It's not a problem."

"But what would the taxpayers say if they knew you were spending time sitting in a park instead of doing your job."

"Keeping you safe is my job. I'll see you there in ten minutes." He hung up.

Peyton loaded up a stroller, several bottles of water for herself and a bottle of formula for Lilly and fought a deep-seated guilt that she was taking him away from his work because she had a touch of cabin fever.

The evening was still warm, but not as stifling hot as it had been earlier in the day. Many times as she'd driven by the park she'd seen mothers and children enjoying the shaded benches and playground equipment. She just wanted to hold Lilly and enjoy the beautiful evening.

The park was located two blocks from the sheriff's office, and as she turned into the parking lot she saw Tom's car already there.

He got out of his car and approached hers and she tried not to notice how handsome he looked in the evening sun.

He looked toward the park, where two women sat on the benches and several children were enjoying the playground equipment.

"See those women?" he asked as she got out of her car.

"That's Dawn Washington and Rachel Cook, two of Black Rock's most upstanding citizens. I've known them both for most of my life. If you want to meet good people, I'll introduce you to them. Then I'll go hang out in the car."

"Tom, I'll be fine here with them. I'll introduce myself. There's no point in you staying here with me. I'll visit with the women and when they leave I'll leave. Nobody is going to try to do anything to me or to Lilly as long as there are other people around. Please, I'd feel better about this whole thing if you'd just go back to the office."

He jammed his hands in his pockets and gazed at the park, then looked at her once again. "You'll leave as they do and go directly home?"

"I promise," she agreed.

"And you'll call me as soon as you get home?"

She nodded and he stepped back from her. "Then I guess you'll be okay." He raised a hand and waved at one of the two women, who waved back. "You'll make friends with them easily," he said to Peyton. "And don't forget to call me when you get home."

She watched as he got into his car. In the best case scenario she would have been sharing the evening in the park with him. They would be sharing dreams, making plans for their future and laughing with Lilly.

"Foolish thoughts," she muttered as she unloaded the stroller, then got Lilly settled in and pushed her toward the two women seated on one of the benches.

"Look at that sweet baby girl," one of them said with a friendly smile.

"Her name is Lilly, and I'm Peyton."

"Hi, Peyton. I'm Dawn, and this is Rachel. Nice to meet you."

Rachel, an attractive blonde looked at Peyton curiously. "Aren't you the woman whose baby was kidnapped?"

Peyton nodded.

"Oh, honey, sit right down here," Dawn exclaimed and made a place between the two for Peyton to sit. "You must have been terrified."

"It was the worst experience I've ever been through," Peyton replied. "Thank goodness Sheriff Grayson managed to find Lilly and return her to me safe and sound."

For the next few minutes they spoke about mothers' fears and shared personal information about themselves.

Dawn was married and had two little boys who were at the moment climbing on the jungle gym. Rachel was also married and the mother of a five-year-old girl who was on the swings.

With Tom's ringing endorsement of the women in her ears it was easier for Peyton to let down her guard just a little bit.

Dawn worked as a secretary in the mayor's office, and Rachel was a stay-at-home mom with a passion for making beaded jewelry.

For Peyton it was delightful to sit and chat with the two women, who were friendly and open and wonderfully ordinary. Rachel was planning a jewelry party in her home and took Peyton's phone number, promising an invite and the opportunity to meet more of the women of Black Rock.

"There's Caleb, making the evening rounds," Dawn said as the deputy's car rolled slowly by the park.

"Those Grayson men definitely got the luck of the hunk genes," Rachel exclaimed. "If I were single I'm not sure which one of their bones I'd jump."

Tom's name jumped right into Peyton's head. "They were all nice while investigating Lilly's kidnapping," she said.

"They're hot, they're nice and they all seem to have an aversion to marriage," Dawn said.

"Sheriff Grayson was married, remember?" Rachel said. "Poor man lost his little girl then his wife left him. I think it broke him completely."

These words pierced through Peyton's heart. Was it

possible that a tragedy like that could break a person so completely he could never love again? Would never seek that kind of happiness again?

If she'd never gotten Lilly back, would that trauma have made her never think about having another child? Would she have never loved anyone that much again?

She liked to think that wasn't the case, that her capacity to love was bigger than anything life could throw her way.

"Well, guess it's time to pack it in," Dawn said. Twilight had fallen, painting the park in violet shadows portending the imminent arrival of night.

She stood from the bench. "Shawn, David, let's go. It's going to take an hour to get the dirt off you before bedtime."

The little boys hollered protests but got off the equipment and headed to their mom as Rachel called for her daughter, Melissa.

"We're here most evenings," Rachel said. "Feel free to join us anytime. Maybe we can do lunch sometime before school starts."

"That would be great," Peyton agreed. As the others began the walk toward their cars, Peyton also got ready to go.

It didn't take long for the other two women to load up their cars while Peyton tried to unfasten the strap holding Lilly in place in the stroller.

It was stuck. She waved goodbye as the others pulled out of the lot and then knelt down to tug on the strap fastener.

"Did you have a good time at the park, Lilly?" She smiled at the baby and leaned down and kissed her cheek, then sighed in relief as she finally managed to get the strap unfastened.

"I think with all this fresh air we should both sleep like babies tonight." She unlocked the back door and placed Lilly in her car seat.

As she fastened her in, Lilly reached out and grabbed her nose and cooed. Peyton laughed and kissed the little hand. "We'll go home and you can have a nice bottle and I'll have a glass of wine. How does that sound?"

Lilly laughed, as if delighted by the plan. As Peyton closed the car door and folded up the stroller to put it in the trunk, she smiled at thoughts of the two women she'd met. They'd been nice, and wonderfully normal.

She thought of Kathy—or India—who had fooled her so completely. Part of the problem, Peyton now recognized, was that she'd isolated herself in the two months after making the move to Black Rock.

She should have been out making lots of friends, she should have had those friends and neighbors to support her when Lilly had been taken. Maybe that's why Tom had become so important, because he'd been the only thing she'd had to hang on to.

She opened the trunk and leaned over to place the stroller inside. As she raised up, something crashed down hard on her back. Her purse fell to the ground, and for a moment she thought that somehow the trunk lid had fallen on her, but she heard the scuffle of footsteps and felt somebody's hot breath on her neck. At the same time a vicious punch in her side sucked her breath away.

She crumbled to the ground, gasping for air. *Get up,* an inner voice screamed inside her head. *You have to get up and protect Lilly.*

Even as the thought exploded in her brain, a foot connected with her ribs and a crashing pain sent stars flying in her head.

She grabbed the fender and attempted to pull herself up and got her first look at her assailant. She couldn't tell anything about him other than he was tall and wore a ski mask that obscured not only his hair color but also any other identifying feature.

"Bitch," he hissed, his voice nothing more than a guttural snarl as he kicked her again...and again.

She tried to scream, but she had no air and she realized he was going to kill her if she didn't move, if she didn't somehow get up.

She tried to crawl away from him. She was light-headed and felt as if she were going to throw up. Still he kicked at her, as if she were a soccer ball he was trying to get through a goal.

"Please," she managed to gasp as her vision blurred and the dark edges of unconsciousness crept closer. *Somebody help me,* she mentally cried, just before the world turned black.

Tom rose from his chair in his office and stretched with his arms overhead. He checked his watch and wondered how long it would be before Peyton called to tell him she was home.

There were moments when he wondered if he were over-reacting to an imagined threat against Peyton. The only person who had hurt her was India, and she was dead. But the fact that there was still a killer out there, a killer who might be connected to Peyton, kept Tom from letting his guard down where she was concerned.

The last three days had yielded no more information on Cliff Gunther, and Tom wondered if maybe the man had been upset that Peyton had begun to date Rick, if perhaps he'd seen Lilly as the final straw?

Since Sunday night with Peyton he'd thrown himself into work. First thing Monday morning he'd gone to the farm where Dr. Larry Norwood, the new vet in town, was now living.

Larry was an affable man, and his wife, Tracy, was just as friendly. They had two beautiful little girls, and it was impossible to imagine Larry risking it all for a woman like India.

They were from Kansas City, and Larry explained that they had been looking for some time to move to a small town where he could focus his practice on farm animals.

He and Dr. Johnson, the man who had been the town vet for the last forty years, had begun to correspond through a Web site. And after months of corresponding, Hank, who was getting ready to retire, encouraged Larry to move to Black Rock and take over his practice.

Although Tom hadn't seriously entertained the

thought that somehow the vet might have something to do with India's death and Lilly's kidnapping, he left the farm feeling that the vet and his family were a nice addition to the town.

He had spent much of the last two days on the phone, working with the Wichita Police Department to investigate some of the people India had associated with while living there.

Along with the growing list of names of lowlifes who had been in India's life before she'd moved to Black Rock, he also was trying to figure out if there was somebody here in town who might have been ripe for an affair, somebody who was capable of murder.

As he shut off the light in his office, his cell phone rang. "Sheriff Grayson," he answered.

"In the park, they're in the park! You need to come right away."

Even though the voice was excited and higher pitched than usual, Tom recognized Walt Toliver. Just what he needed to round out the day—a call from the local eccentric.

"Walt, calm down," Tom said. "What's in the park?"

"It was an alien, and he hurt a woman. You got to get out here, Sheriff, she's hurt bad, and the baby won't stop crying."

A burst of adrenaline shot through Tom. Walt called on a regular basis to talk about the alien invasion he thought was taking place in and around the Black Rock area, but Peyton had been in the park with Lilly.

"Is the alien still there?" he asked as he left his office.

"No, I chased him off, but the woman is on the ground and somebody needs to do something about that poor baby. Just listen to that crying." Walt must have held out the phone, for in the background Tom could hear the faint cries of an infant.

"Walt, I'm on my way." Tom clicked off and looked at Sam and Benjamin, who were sitting at their desks. "Benjamin, come with me. That was Walt, and he said somebody needs help in the park. Peyton was there earlier. I think she's in trouble." His heart crashed with rapid beats as he raced out of the office.

Within minutes they were in Tom's car and headed to the park. As he drove, Tom quickly filled Benjamin in on what Walt had said.

As the park came into sight and Tom saw the familiar car parked in the lot, his heart felt as if it had exploded in his chest.

Peyton!

He pulled the car to a halt several yards away from hers and jumped out of it with his heart pumping frantically.

Walt was pacing at the back of the vehicle, where Tom could see Peyton crumpled on the ground. The sound of Lilly's wails filled the air.

"I was afraid to move her," Walt said as Tom raced to her side.

"Benjamin, get Lilly and call for an ambulance," he said as he knelt down beside Peyton. "Peyton, can you hear me?" Oh, God, she looked so small, so utterly broken.

Her eyelids fluttered and opened. She stared up at him for a moment with bewilderment, then her eyes filled with horror. "Lilly!" she cried and tried to rise, but she groaned with the movement and collapsed back on the ground.

"Don't try to move," Tom said quickly. "Lilly is fine. Benjamin is getting her out of her car seat. We'll take care of her." She closed her eyes and for a moment he thought she'd lost consciousness again.

"He was kicking her, the alien was," Walt exclaimed. "I thought they might be landing in the park tonight so I came out here to check it out, and that's when I saw him attacking her."

Benjamin had Lilly in his arms and was walking with her. She'd stopped crying so the only sounds were those of Peyton's labored breathing and Walt's footsteps as he paced in the dry grass.

"I was putting the stroller in the trunk," Peyton said, her voice achingly weak. "He came up behind me and hit me in the back."

"Did you recognize him?" Tom asked.

"He had no face," Walt said, obviously overexcited. "He was one of those outer-space creatures without any features."

"He had on a ski mask," Peyton said. "I don't know who it was. I don't know what he wanted." A sob escaped her and she reached for Tom's hand. "I think he meant to kill me. He just kept kicking and kicking."

"Shh, don't try to talk," Tom said, his heart breaking as he saw the pain she was in. There would be questions for her later, after she'd been treated.

He released her hand and stood as the ambulance arrived. Thankfully they hadn't used the siren, which probably would have traumatized Lilly.

As the paramedics loaded Peyton, Tom assured her that he'd be at the hospital with Lilly as soon as possible. As the ambulance drove away he picked up her purse, which she'd dropped in the attack, detached the baby seat from the back and installed it in his car, then locked her vehicle.

"Benjamin, take a statement from Walt and call Sam and Caleb to start canvassing the area. I'll take the baby and head over to the hospital."

As he took Lilly from Benjamin, he tried to ignore the sweet memory of another baby in his arms. He quickly fastened her into the car seat, then got in behind the steering wheel.

What in the hell was going on in his town? He clenched the steering wheel hard as he headed to the small local hospital. Who had attacked Peyton, and why? Was there something about her past that she hadn't told him? Beneath the questions lingered a killing guilt. Why had he allowed her to go to the park? Why hadn't he stayed with her?

A million questions flew through his head as he parked the car and got Lilly out of the backseat. The baby had fallen asleep, and for that Tom was grateful.

The loudest question that pounded in his head was

about Peyton's condition. She hadn't been able to move without groaning. What kind of internal damage had been done?

The idea of any man laying his hands or his feet on her filled him with rage. She was so small, so fragile. And why would anyone want to hurt her?

He walked through the emergency room door, but before he could get much farther, he was stopped by Loretta McCain, Sam's wife.

"Whoa," she said as she stepped between him and the door leading to the exam rooms. "Where do you think you're going, and where did you get that precious bundle of love?"

"I need to check in on Peyton Wilkerson. She was just brought in, and this is Lilly, her daughter."

"You know you can't go back there right now. The doctor is with her. I'm sure he'll come out to speak to you after he's had a chance to check her out." She smiled at the sleeping baby, her chocolate eyes twinkling with a maternal light. "You want me to take that little bundle from you? I can put her in one of our bassinettes until we figure out what's going on."

"That's a great idea," he said, eager to relinquish the baby, who smelled of baby powder and innocence and a million old memories.

As Loretta disappeared with Lilly, Tom sank down on one of the molded plastic chairs to wait for an update from the doctor. He knew Benjamin and Caleb would be taking care of the investigation, which was good, because all Tom could think about at the moment was Peyton's well-being.

Every time he thought of her on the ground at the back of her car he felt sick to his stomach. He wanted to hurt somebody. He wanted to find the man responsible and smash in his face. It was definitely not the thoughts of a sheriff, but rather those of a man whose woman had been hurt.

It felt as if hours passed before Dr. Ryan Attenburg came into the waiting room. Tom leapt out of his chair. "How is she?"

"Two cracked ribs and a multitude of bruises, but other than that she's okay."

Tom inwardly cringed as he imagined the power of the kicks that had cracked her ribs. "You're releasing her?"

"I've got her bound up and with a prescription for some pain meds. There isn't much more I can do for her. She's going to feel like hell for a while, but it's just going to take time to heal."

"Can I go back and see her?"

"While you do that, I'll just get her discharge papers ready."

There were only three examining rooms in the emergency area, and she was in the first. He pushed the curtain back to see her seated on the table, her arms wrapped around her midsection and her face as pale as the bleached cotton gown she wore.

She looked up at him and her eyes widened. "Lilly? Where's Lilly?"

"It's okay. She's with one of the nurses."

"Oh, God, was she hurt?" Tears instantly jumped into her eyes.

"No, no. She's fine," Tom hurriedly assured her. "She fell asleep, so one of the nurses put her in one of the cribs in the nursery."

She released a small sigh. "What's going on, Tom? Why would somebody do this to me? It wasn't a robbery attempt. I dropped my purse the minute he struck me from behind."

"I don't know, but I swear I'm going to find who did this to you." He would move heaven and earth to put the guilty behind bars. It was all connected, the kidnapping of Lilly and this assault on Peyton. Somebody was after Peyton, and that somebody had killed India.

A young nurse's aide appeared in the doorway. "I'm here to help you get dressed, Ms. Wilkerson."

"I'll just wait outside. I'll take you home when you're ready." Tom left and returned to the waiting room, where he called Benjamin for an update.

Unfortunately, he had nothing to report. He could get nothing out of Walt except that it had been a tall alien with no face. The assailant had run down the street when Walt had hollered at him, but there was no sign of anyone in or around the area. They had knocked on the doors of the houses in the vicinity, but nobody had seen or heard anything.

So Tom was left with nothing but an eyewitness who watched the heavens for alien spaceships and believed an invasion from outer space was imminent.

Loretta appeared with a still-sleeping Lilly in her
arms. "You best be carrying this one out. Her mama
isn't going to feel like lifting anything for a couple of
days."

As Tom took the infant into his arms, Peyton walked
through the double doors with the doctor. She walked
with tiny steps, as if every bone in her body hurt.

Once again a slow, seething rage built up inside Tom.
He wanted to envelop her in bubble wrap, lock her in a
padded room, do whatever it took to make sure nobody
and nothing could hurt her again.

"I've given her some samples of pain meds since
the drugstore is closed for the night. She has enough to
last until tomorrow," Dr. Attenburg said. He turned and
offered a sympathetic smile to Peyton. "I have a feeling
you're going to feel like you've been run over by a truck
when you wake up in the morning."

"What I'd like more than anything right now is my
bed and a handful of those pain pills," she said.

"Let's get you home," Tom said.

It took several minutes to get Lilly back into the
infant car seat and Peyton loaded into the passenger
side. She leaned her head back and closed her eyes as
Tom got into the car and started the engine.

"Can you talk about it?" he asked as they left the
hospital parking lot. She opened her eyes and nodded.

"I had trouble unfastening the clasp on the stroller.
By the time I got it unhooked and got Lilly into the car,
the other women had left. I had just put the stroller in the
trunk when I was hit from behind. Then it all happened

so fast. I was on the ground and he was kicking me over and over again."

"Did he say anything to you?"

"No...oh wait, yes. He called me a bitch, but it was a deep snarl. I didn't recognize the voice. All I could think about was that he was going to kill me and take Lilly."

Guilt ripped through him. "Is that what you think it was about? He wanted to get Lilly?"

"I can't imagine what it was about. All I know is that if Walt hadn't been in that park, I'd be dead." She wrapped her arms around her middle as if seeking warmth.

Tom pulled into her driveway and cut the engine. As she got out of the car he pulled Lilly from her car seat. She was awake and her big blue eyes met his and a smile curved her little lips.

Tom steeled his heart against that baby smile as he and Peyton walked to the front door. Peyton carried the purse Tom had retrieved from the scene and she dug into it to find her keys.

"You need to go directly to bed," Tom said once they were inside the house.

"I need to give Lilly a bottle before I do anything," she replied. She moved slowly toward the kitchen, and Tom followed just behind her with Lilly still in his arms.

"She can sleep with me tonight," Peyton said as she fixed a bottle. "That way if she wakes up for any reason I don't have to get out of bed."

"She can sleep in her own bed," Tom said. "If she wakes up or needs anything, I'll be here. What you need most is uninterrupted rest, and if I know you, you won't take those pain pills because you're afraid Lilly might need you in the night."

"You shouldn't have to stay and babysit me through the night," she protested, but he thought he saw a hint of relief in her eyes.

"I'm not just staying through the night," Tom said. "I'm staying here until we figure out exactly what's going on." He hesitated a moment, then decided to give it to her straight. She'd proven herself to be a strong individual, and he needed her to be aware of just what was at stake here.

"If what you said was true, and you really believe that man's intention tonight was to kill you, then he was unsuccessful," he said.

She looked at him for a long moment, and the relief that had momentarily lit her eyes was replaced with a tinge of fear. "You think he'll be back."

It was a statement, not a question, and Tom simply nodded his head as Lilly began to cry in his arms.

Chapter 10

When Peyton awakened the next morning she didn't feel as if she'd been hit by a truck. She felt as if a hundred trucks had smashed into her.

A glance at her clock let her know it was just after six. The sun was just beginning to peek over the horizon, and she knew Lilly would probably sleep for another hour or so.

She closed her eyes again, not wanting to move, not wanting to breathe as each and every inch of her body ached.

He had wanted her dead. She'd felt it in the fierceness of the attack, in the hatred that had oozed from him. *Why?* That was the single question that kept replaying in her mind.

Why would somebody want her dead? Who hated

her so much to do something like this to her? A week ago she would have said she had no enemies, but if that were the case, then what had the attack been about? It had felt personal. The way he had growled "bitch" had definitely felt personal.

She shut her eyes and tried to think of somebody, anybody close to her who might harbor that kind of hatred. Rick? Impossible. They had moved on with their lives without any real entanglements, without any bitterness.

She'd worked a lot of jobs, met a lot of people before moving to Black Rock. Had there been somebody she'd angered?

Buck Harmon. The name jumped into her mind. Had he been more angry than she thought when she'd bumped his truck with her shopping cart? It seemed crazy to think that an incident like that could result in the vicious attack on her.

And then there was Cliff. She'd been dating him, although not seriously, when she'd met Rick. Had Cliff been more serious about her than she'd thought? Serious enough that he'd gone off the deep end and now wanted to hurt her?

With her thoughts making her head pound, she decided it was counterproductive to stay in bed and worry about questions with no answers.

Gingerly, she sat up, stifling a moan. A hot shower. Maybe that would help ease the bumps and bruises that covered her body.

She eased her feet over the edge of the bed and stood,

slowly making her way into the adjoining bathroom. She unwrapped the loose binding that the doctor had wrapped around her and gasped as she saw the black-and-blue marks that mottled her torso.

A few minutes later as she stood beneath a hot spray of water she thought about the fact that apparently Tom was going to be her houseguest for a while. She'd wanted to spend more time with him, but certainly not under these circumstances.

She'd hoped he'd want to spend more time with her, but it was duty and responsibility and not desire and attraction that had him back in her life.

Once she stepped out of the shower she dried carefully, then pulled on a pair of shorts and a short-sleeved blouse. A regular bra was impossible with the soreness of her ribs, but she managed to get on an old, stretched-out sports bra.

As she walked down the hall she smelled the scent of coffee and knew that Tom was awake. To her surprise, when she walked into the kitchen she saw Lilly, looking fresh and happy in her bouncy chair on the table.

Tom scowled at her as she walked into the kitchen and eased down into a chair. "You were supposed to stay in bed." He pulled a cup out of the cabinet and poured her coffee.

"I tried, but I woke up, and my thoughts started giving me a headache. Thanks," she added as she wrapped her fingers around the cup.

"You want a pain pill?"

"No, I'm okay as long as I don't move too fast or try

to breathe too deeply." She took a sip of her coffee then reached out a hand and grabbed Lilly's fingers. "How's my girl this morning?"

"I gave her a bottle and changed her," Tom said as he joined her at the table.

"I think that goes above and beyond your duties as a sheriff."

He frowned. "Yeah, well, I don't seem to be doing so well with my sheriff duties. No matter how I twist it all around, I can't make sense of anything that's happened."

"Trying to make sense of it is what gave me a headache before I got out of bed this morning," she replied.

Even though her body ached and her head pounded, a tiny flutter of pleasure swept through her as she smelled the familiar scent of him, felt the warmth of his eyes lingering on her.

She was not a foolish woman, but she felt foolish now, like a teenager with a crush on a boy when she had no hopes of winning his heart.

But there was something about Tom that made her believe his heart needed to be claimed again, that he was a man who not only needed, but deserved to be loved.

"I had Benjamin bring your car home last night," he said.

The ring of the phone swallowed her murmur of thanks. Tom jumped up and grabbed the cordless and handed it to her.

"Peyton, are you all right?" Rick's voice burst over

the line. "They told me somebody beat the hell out of you."

"I'm okay," she replied. "Who told you about it?"

"Benjamin Grayson called this morning to ask me where I was last night. I told him I was here in my apartment writing arguments for the trial I'm working, and he told me about the attack on you. Jesus, Peyton, what's going on there?"

"I wish I knew," she replied and watched as Tom left the room.

"Are you sure you're okay?" Rick asked.

"I'm fine, Rick. A little frightened, a little banged up, but I'm okay."

"Maybe you should come back here, stay with me for a while. I have plenty of room for you and Lilly, and I'd feel better if I knew you were here safe and sound."

A burst of warmth swept through her at his offer. Life would have been so much less complicated if they had truly loved each other. But she didn't love him and he didn't love her, at least not in a romantic way.

"I appreciate the offer, Rick, but I'm not going anywhere. I'm confident Sheriff Grayson will figure this all out soon and I can get back to a normal life."

"Do you need anything? Is there anything I can do for you? For Lilly?" he asked.

"We're fine, and we have everything we need," she replied.

"Call me if there's anything I can do. I mean it, Peyton. All you have to do is let me know."

"Thanks, Rick. I appreciate it."

They hung up and Peyton got up from the table to go in search of Tom. He was in the living room, standing by the front window and staring outside.

For a moment she simply stood and looked at him, noting the width of his broad shoulders, the way his khaki slacks fit across his tight butt.

He must have sensed her presence, for he turned around to face her. His features held stress, and she wanted to stroke her fingers across the lines in his forehead until they smoothed out.

"You had Benjamin check out Rick's alibi for last night?" she said.

Tom nodded. "If you knew the pope personally, I'd be having Benjamin check his alibi."

"I think it's safe to mark the pope off our list of suspects," she said in an attempt to bring a smile to his face. It didn't work.

"I was just thinking that it would be a good idea for you to get an alarm system installed," he said. "I could have somebody out here by this afternoon if you agree."

"At this point I think it would be a good idea," she replied. It would also allow him to leave her and get back to his work.

As much as she'd love to have him as a personal bodyguard, he was the sheriff and couldn't spend the rest of his life living here with her. There was a tiny part inside her that wished he could spend the rest of his life with her, not as a bodyguard but as a man who loved her.

"I'll make a phone call and get somebody out here as soon as possible," he said. "In the meantime, I've got Caleb coming over to sit with you while I take care of some business. I'll pick up your pain meds while I'm out. I don't want you leaving this house for anything right now."

As she looked into his somber dark eyes, it struck her just how serious this was, that somebody wanted her dead and might try to kill her again.

"Tom, what's happened to my life?" she asked softly. "Why is this happening to me?"

For a brief moment she thought he was going to take her in his arms, but instead he shoved his hands into his pockets and rocked back on his heels. "I don't know, Peyton. Is there anything you haven't told me, about yourself, about your relationship with Rick? Anything about past coworkers or friends that might explain this? Any old boyfriends before Rick besides Cliff?"

"No. Just Cliff, and that's it. That's what I was thinking about before I got out of bed this morning. I've racked my brain trying to figure out who might want to hurt me, and I can't think of anyone."

As Lilly wailed from the kitchen, Peyton left the living room and went back to where the little girl was in her infant seat.

Tom followed behind her and watched as she took Lilly from the seat and sat with the baby in one of the kitchen chairs. She fought the wince of pain that stabbed through her as Lilly snuggled against her ribs.

"Have you checked out Buck Harmon's alibi for last night?" she asked.

He nodded. "Apparently Buck was home alone last night, not exactly an airtight alibi. I've got Sam McCain going over the area in the park with a fine-tooth comb, looking for any evidence the attacker might have left behind, but I'm not very confident that he'll find anything. Right now the only thing we can do is to suspect everyone and trust nobody."

She sighed and stroked her fingers through Lilly's downy hair. "This is not exactly the way I want to live my life."

"This isn't going to last the rest of your life," he replied. "Whoever attacked you last night wants you dead, and I have a gut feeling that he's going to try again. Hopefully, sooner or later, he'll show his hand, make a mistake that will let us know who he is, but in the meantime the only thing we can do is stay on the defensive."

Peyton hugged Lilly tighter to her, fighting against the chill of fear that snaked up her spine.

By four o'clock that afternoon a security system had been installed in Peyton's house. Nobody would be able to get in through a window or door without an alarm sounding.

Dawn Washington and Rachel Cook, her new friends from the park, had stopped by just after noon, having heard the news about the attack on Peyton. Tom took the opportunity to question them both, but unfortunately they hadn't seen anyone suspicious lurking around the area, nor had they seen a vehicle approaching as they left.

Tom's frustration over the case was complicated by his frustration over his feelings where Peyton was concerned. He cared about her deeply, but taking care of Lilly that morning had only confirmed his desire to remain alone.

As he'd changed Lilly and heard her soft coos and baby laughter, memories of Kelly had played in his head, and the old familiar pain had filled his heart.

But the toughest thing he did all day was keep his hands off Peyton. There were moments in the day when he'd wanted to wrap his arms around her bruised and battered body, when he'd wanted to kiss the fear out of her eyes, but he hadn't.

He'd left the house for a couple of hours after Caleb had arrived and had picked up Peyton's pain meds, then he had gone to the office to check in.

The fact that still nobody had heard from Brittany added an additional fragment of worry in the back of his head. She'd disappeared before for as long as a week, but this was the longest time she'd been gone with no contact.

He could only hope that she was safe and sound. He had no reason to think otherwise, and besides, he already had plenty to deal with, like finding whoever wanted Peyton dead.

He'd returned to Peyton's place and sent Caleb back to the office, and now he sat in the kitchen while she fixed a salad and broiled a couple of steaks. Lilly was in her swing, smiling at Tom whenever she caught his eye, filling him with the memories of another family, another life.

Peyton was different than Julie. Julie had been needy, a woman who had required lots of attention and energy. Tom hadn't minded giving it to her because he'd loved her. But if he was perfectly honest with himself, when she'd walked out on him there had been a little bit of relief. It had taken every ounce of his energy to try to assuage her guilt and to shoulder her grief over Kelly's death.

He'd made up his mind to spend another night with Peyton. Even with the security system, he wasn't comfortable leaving her and Lilly alone.

"Rare, medium or well done?" she asked as she bent over to check the steaks. She winced as she straightened back up.

"Rare. Have you taken any of those pills I picked up for you?"

She shook her head. "I don't like to take pain medicine. I don't have any tolerance for it. It makes me groggy and out of it."

"I don't like to see you in pain," he said gruffly.

"It's okay, it's manageable at the moment. I might take a pill at bedtime, but in the past they've always hit me so hard."

"You know, if you take a pain pill when you need it, it doesn't make you a drug addict like your mother," he said.

She looked at him sharply as if he'd suddenly dived into her innermost fears. She set the bowl of salad on the table and sat in the chair opposite him. "Maybe I am a little afraid of that," she admitted.

"You aren't your mother, Peyton, and there's no reason for you not to treat the pain. It's one thing to try to be strong, but it's another to martyr yourself for no good reason."

"Okay, you win. After dinner I'll take a pill," she replied. "It's already seven, and by the time we finish eating I'll put Lilly down and feel more comfortable taking one."

As they ate the meal Tom tried to keep the conversation off the crime. He couldn't help but notice that with every hour that passed her features tightened with the pain from her ribs.

After dinner he cleared the dishes while she gave Lilly a bottle. Once Lilly had been fed he brought her a glass of water and two of the pain pills.

"Take these, and I want no arguments," he said firmly. "I can tell that you're hurting badly."

To his surprise she took the pills and swallowed them without protest. That, as much as the strained look on her face, let him know she was hurting more than she was letting on.

By eight-thirty Lilly was down for the night and Peyton was loopy from the pills. Tom had never seen anything like it before. He'd never seen anyone with less tolerance.

"I feel good enough to go dancing," she said. She

was half slumped on the sofa and her eyes were half closed.

Tom couldn't help but smile at her. "I think it's time you danced right into your bed."

She released a deep sigh. "Maybe you're right," she agreed. As she stood from the sofa she swayed, and Tom quickly jumped up and grabbed her before she could fall.

"Whoa," he exclaimed. "You weren't kidding when you said you have no tolerance."

She leaned heavily against him. "I told you I shouldn't take those silly pills." A giggle escaped her lips. "Those silly little pills make me just a little bit silly."

For just a moment all the tension that the day had brought fell aside as he looked into Peyton's laughing eyes. He was surprised by the chuckle that escaped him. "At the moment, you look smashed."

She nodded. "I feel smashed. Help me to bed?"

Every muscle in Tom's body tensed. He'd love to help her to bed. He'd love to stretch out next to her and take her in his arms and make love to her through the long, lonely night.

But of course he wouldn't do that. "Sure," he said. "Let's get you tucked in safe and sound."

He helped her to the bedroom, where she sat on the edge of the bed like a helpless child. He watched her as she fumbled unsuccessfully to unbutton her blouse.

"Let me help." He leaned down and quickly unfastened the buttons and tried not to breathe in the scent of her, a fresh, feminine fragrance that always stirred him.

Still, his blood heated in his veins and he mentally chastised himself for wanting a woman who was dopey on pain meds and hurting.

He pushed the blouse off her shoulders, and it fell to the bed behind her. He saw the dark bruises that covered her skin beginning beneath the band of her bra and disappearing into the waist of her shorts; a deep moan escaped him.

The sight of the ugly bruises threatened to bring tears to his eyes as emotion swelled up inside him. Although he'd known she was hurt, knowing and seeing were two different things.

"Peyton, I'm sorry. I'm so sorry." His voice was thick as he fought to control his emotion.

She placed her hands on either side of his face and forced him to look at her. "Don't be sad, Tom. It's okay. I'm okay. The bruises will heal, and at least I'm alive, but I don't want you to be sad."

She awed him, this woman who had been beaten up and might have been killed but didn't want him to be sad. "Let's get you into bed," he said.

Her nightgown was laid out on the nearby chair, and as she stood to remove her shorts he retrieved the gown. As she finished undressing to put on her nightgown, Tom averted his gaze from her and turned down the bed covers.

As she slid in beneath the sheets, she looked at him with a soft gaze. "Sleep with me, Tom?"

He wanted to tell her no, that there was no way he wanted to be next to her in the bed, smelling the scent of her, feeling her body heat. And yet he couldn't tell her no with those sleepy blue eyes gazing at him.

She was traumatized and she was drugged, and he knew if he just slipped into the bed next to her she'd probably be asleep within two minutes.

He kicked off his shoes, took off his shirt and pulled off his slacks and slid beneath the sheet next to her.

She sighed, as if at peace, and placed her small, warm hand over his chest and almost immediately fell asleep.

He realized he could love her if he allowed himself to. But as he thought of Lilly and family, his chest tightened as if squeezed by a steel vise.

He could love her, but he wouldn't. He'd catch the person responsible for the attack, the person he believed still posed a threat, then he'd walk out of her life and never look back.

Chapter 11

Peyton awoke the next morning feeling worse than she had the day before. Dawn hadn't yet lightened the eastern sky, and a quick look at her clock told her it was just after five.

She closed her eyes and tried to go back to sleep, but her body ached too badly and she was completely awake. She pulled on a robe and left the bedroom.

As quietly as possible, she went down the hallway, stopping first in Lilly's doorway to see her sleeping peacefully. She went on down the hall and stopped at the doorway of the living room, where Tom was asleep on the sofa.

She had a vague memory of him in the bed next to her the night before. He must have gotten up and moved here at some point after she'd fallen asleep.

The room was lit by the light over the sink in the kitchen drifting in, and she took a moment just to watch him sleep.

He couldn't be comfortable, with his feet hanging over the foot of the sofa and his head crammed into the corner. He had her spare pillow beneath his head and a sheet pulled halfway up his bare chest.

Even in sleep he touched her on a physical and mental level. She had a vague memory of his tenderness the night before when he'd helped her get ready for bed.

She was certain he had a great capacity to love, but he seemed intent on denying that in his life. Had the death of his child and the abandonment by his wife left him so damaged he could never reach out for love again? If that were so, then that would be the real tragedy in his life.

"Couldn't sleep?"

The deep voice startled her and she jumped in surprise. "How did you know I was here?"

"Just sensed you." He sat up and raked a hand through his tousled hair. "How do you feel?"

She frowned. "Worse today than I did yesterday," she admitted.

"They say the second day after an accident is always the worst."

She'd never seen him look as sexy as he did now, with his hair bed-tousled and his bare chest staring her in the face. The aches and pains that shot through her didn't stop the flicker of desire that roared to life.

In that moment she recognized that as crazy as it was,

she'd fallen in love with Sheriff Tom Grayson. It didn't matter that they'd known each other only a short period of time; it didn't matter than they hadn't even dated. She knew what was in her heart, in her soul, and it was love for this man.

"I'm going to go put on the coffee," she said, suddenly needing to be away from him. She escaped into the kitchen and started the coffee, then sat at the kitchen table and thought about Tom Grayson.

Loving him was probably a study in futility, and yet she couldn't help the tiny flicker of hope that burned in her heart.

Despite his firm words to her that he had no intention of getting involved with anyone again, she knew he cared about her, knew he cared about her more than he might be willing to admit.

But did he care enough that he'd want to pursue a relationship with her after all this madness had ended? She hoped so. She was sipping a cup of the fresh brew when he came into the kitchen.

He'd showered and was dressed in a clean uniform. His hair was neatly combed, and as he walked over to pour himself a cup of coffee she couldn't help but admire his attractiveness. But it was his inner qualities that drew her, his gentleness and intelligence, his ability to comfort and offer support under the worst of circumstances.

He got his coffee then joined her at the table, and she saw that despite the shower he looked tired. "You can't have slept well on the sofa," she said.

"I'm okay," he replied.

She drew a deep breath. "You could have stayed in bed with me."

"I didn't think that was a good idea. I might have accidentally jostled you in the night." He gazed at her a moment, then focused outside the nearby window—but not before she saw the flare of heat in his eyes. His mouth might say one thing to her, but his eyes told her something else altogether.

She wanted to tell him that she was in love with him, but she knew the timing wasn't right. He had India's murder and the attack on her on his mind. There wasn't space for her to speak her mind to him. She had a feeling it would only add to his burden. Eventually there would be a time when she could speak to him from her heart; she just knew that time wasn't now.

Peyton had just finished her cup of coffee when she heard the sound of Lilly awaken. She left the kitchen and went into the nursery to take care of her daughter.

Lilly greeted her with a happy smile, and as she changed her diaper, love filled Peyton's heart. From the moment she'd realized she was pregnant with her daughter, Peyton had prepared herself for being a single parent.

She knew how to be alone. She'd been alone most of her life, but there was a difference in knowing you would be okay alone and wanting something different.

She wanted Tom in her life, not just as a sheriff protecting her but as a man loving her. For the first time in her life she felt a need inside her where another human being was concerned, and that scared her more than just a little bit.

Once she had Lilly changed, she carried her back into the kitchen, where Tom was already on his cell phone. She placed the baby in the infant seat then made a bottle as he walked into the living room to complete his call.

When he returned to the kitchen, she was sitting and feeding Lilly her bottle. As much as she felt safe with him here, as much as she wanted him here with her day and night, night and day, she was struck by the fact that as sheriff he shouldn't be holed up in her house; he should be in his office taking care of business.

"Tom, if I had my way I'd have you living here forever." She felt the heat of a blush warm her cheeks as she realized perhaps her words gave too much away of what was in her heart.

"But you have a job and I know you can't do it effectively playing bodyguard here to me," she continued. "I have the alarm system and I feel relatively safe here. You need to get back to work, in your office. Find the man who killed India. Find the man who attacked me. That's your job, not babysitting me."

He walked over to the coffeepot and poured himself a cup, then turned to face her. "You'd have to agree not to leave the house for anything. If you or Lilly need something, anything, then you have to promise to call me and I'll take care of it."

"I can do that," she agreed. "Trust me, after what happened to me at the park, I'm not eager to leave this house for anything."

He took a sip of his coffee, his gaze remaining on her. "I've got my men working on various angles of both crimes. I'll hang out here until noon and see where we are with everything."

She nodded, pleased that she would have him with her for another half a day.

The morning passed all too quickly. As Lilly went down for her morning nap, Peyton made breakfast for her and Tom.

As they ate they talked about everything but the crimes. They talked about favorite foods and old movies, they spoke of the predictions of a harsh winter to come and the hot summer still here.

Each and every fact she learned about him only solidified her feelings for him. They were alike in the ways that mattered and not alike in ways that would be stimulating and exciting.

There was a part of her that believed that fate had somehow brought them together, that he was a man who needed to love and she and Lilly had all the love in the world to give to him.

But at noon as he prepared to leave, she realized it was equally possible that fate was toying with her, bringing into her life a man she loved but who would never allow himself to become a part of her life.

"I'm not entirely comfortable leaving you here alone," he said at the front door. "I'll make sure a squad car comes by periodically to make sure everything is all right."

"The security system will do the job, and besides,

how long can you be my bodyguard and let all the other business of Black Rock fall by the wayside?"

"You promise you'll call me if you need anything," he asked.

"I promise," she replied.

"And you'll take a pain pill if you need it?" He raised a hand, as if to touch her face, but then quickly dropped it back to his side. "You look like you need one."

She forced a smile to her face. "I'm fine. If I need one later I'll take one. You'll keep me posted on what's happening with the investigation?"

"Of course," he replied as he opened the front door.

She wanted to tell him she had fallen in love with him, but she was afraid to bare her soul to a man who she suspected was at this very moment telling her goodbye.

"Lock the door and set the alarm when I leave," he said.

She nodded. "I will."

His eyes were dark, fathomless, as he gazed at her. "We'll get him, Peyton, and hopefully very soon you'll be able to get back to your real life."

He didn't wait for her to reply, and she watched as he walked down the sidewalk and got into his car. As he pulled out of the driveway, an emptiness filled her.

Maybe she'd have the chance to tell him that she loved him after this was all over. When India's killer was in jail and Peyton's attacker had been caught, then maybe Tom's heart would be open to her.

* * *

Tom drove away from Peyton's and drew a deep, long breath of relief. He'd been on edge all night after helping her into bed, and that same tension had filled his chest all morning.

It was as if his body and his brain had disconnected where Peyton was concerned. He always figured he'd spend the rest of his life alone, and yet every time he looked at Peyton, each time she was close to him, a sweeping desire soared inside him.

It was more than the desire to make love to her, although that particular want roared through him with an intensity that stunned him.

The problem was he liked waking up to her presence, to that beautiful smile that warmed him from the top of his head to the tip of his toes. He liked sharing his first cup of coffee of the day with her, talking to her about everything and nothing.

If he looked deep in his heart, he'd even admit that he was charmed by Lilly, who rarely had a cranky moment and seemed to spend most of her days bestowing smiles on whoever came near.

"Crazy love," he muttered as he pulled into the parking space in front of his office. Surely that's all it was, a false sense of closeness induced by what they'd been through together.

He could never give her what she was looking for in a man, and in any case he wasn't willing to try. She needed a man whose heart was unfettered by loss, a man who could make her and Lilly number one in his life.

He got out of his car and tried to push thoughts of her out of his mind. He had work to do, and there was no question he'd do it better from his office than from Peyton's house.

What he needed more than anything was physical distance from her, and escaping into his office and work was what he did best.

Sam greeted him as he came in the door. "Hey, boss. I didn't know you were coming in today."

"I can't bodyguard for Peyton Wilkerson for the rest of my life. The best thing to do is figure out who's responsible and get them behind bars. But tell Caleb and Benjamin I want them to rotate hourly drive-bys on her house."

Sam nodded. "Done. On that note, I've got two things to tell you. I managed to track down Cliff Gunther. He's at his parents' home in Arizona, has been there since walking out on his job."

"So, he couldn't be responsible for the attack on Peyton."

Sam nodded. "Also, Benjamin is out interviewing one of Buck's neighbors. The neighbor says he saw India Richards's car parked at Buck's on more than one occasion."

"So Buck lied about hanging with India just one night. Gee, why am I not surprised?" Tom frowned thoughtfully. "Get Caleb to meet Benjamin at Buck's place. I want him brought in for questioning. Maybe sitting in our little interrogation room he'll feel more like telling the truth. And, Sam, I want you to do your magic on the computer and get me everything you can find on Rick Powell." From the moment Tom had met Rick, something hadn't felt right. Now he had a hunch that might or might not play out.

"Done," Sam replied. He was on the phone before Tom entered his own office.

Tom closed the door and at his desk pulled out the files on both crimes that were uppermost in his mind. He opened the file for India's murder. He'd read through it over a dozen times but hoped that this time he'd see something he'd missed.

He didn't know how long he'd been sitting studying the files, when their guest of honor arrived. Buck Harmon filled the air with a string of expletives as he was led to the interrogation room next to Tom's office.

A moment late Caleb poked his head in Tom's door and offered him a grin. "He's here, and he's not happy."

"He'll be even less happy after I'm finished with him," Tom replied as he got up from his desk.

There had been a rage in Tom since the moment he'd arrived at the park and had seen Peyton on the ground, and even though he'd managed to stuff that rage down for the last couple of days, he felt it now rising up inside him.

He couldn't help but think that the kidnapping, the murder and the attack on Peyton were all related; he just hadn't been able to figure out the missing link. Was Buck that link?

Time to find out what Buck was hiding and why.

As Tom entered the interrogation room with Benjamin, Buck glared at him with belligerent defiance.

"What the hell, Sheriff? What's going on?"

"We need to have a little chat, Buck," Tom said, his voice deceptively friendly. "You want something to drink? Maybe a coffee or something?"

"All I want is to get out of here," Buck replied. "Ask me whatever you need to so I can get out of here."

Tom eased down in the chair next to Buck at the table while Benjamin stood guard at the door. "India Richards," Tom said.

"We already had that talk," Buck exclaimed as he averted his gaze from Tom's.

"I think maybe you left some things out," Tom replied. "You told me that you'd only seen India one night, but we have witnesses that place her car at your place more than one night."

Buck shot up straighter in his chair. "Then they're lying."

"And why would your neighbors lie about you?" Tom asked.

Buck snorted, as if the answer were obvious to any idiot. "They think my truck is too loud and my place is an eyesore."

"And so they would lie to get you into trouble," Tom said, his voice filled with his disbelief. He stood with an abruptness that made Buck jump in surprise. "He doesn't want to play nice, so I guess I won't, either," he said to Benjamin. "Book him on murder charges."

"Whoa, wait a minute." Buck shot out of his chair

and Benjamin stepped forward, his gun drawn. Buck instantly raised his hands above his head to show he meant no menace. "Okay, okay. I'll tell you the truth." He eased back down in the chair and looked up at Tom.

Tom sat back at the table. "I'm listening."

"It's true that I met her down at Harley's and after we left there we stopped and bought some more beer and hung out at my place. After that she'd sometimes just drop in to talk and have a beer. We weren't having sex. It was nothing like that. She told me she had a boyfriend and wasn't going to cheat on him. I just got the feeling she was lonely."

"Why didn't you tell me all this when I first asked you about her?" Tom asked.

"I don't exactly have the best reputation around these parts," he said dryly. "I'd heard she'd kidnapped a kid, then had been murdered and I didn't want to be involved in any of it."

"You are involved, Buck, whether you want to be or not." Tom leaned back in his chair and eyed the young man across from him.

His mind filled with a vision of Peyton's ribs, black and blue from somebody kicking her with a bone-crushing force. He looked down to the boots Buck wore, and the rage he'd been fighting rose to the surface.

"Maybe you were worried that Peyton Wilkerson knew you were friends with India." He stood once again and leaned over Buck, invading his personal space. "Maybe you saw her the other night in the park and figured you could keep her from telling that you and India were friendly with each other."

A red haze fell before Tom's eyes. "Is that what happened, Buck?" Tom grabbed the front of his shirt and half pulled him from the chair. "Were you afraid that Peyton might know too much, and so you shoved her to the ground and kicked her over and over again?"

"Tom, that's enough." Benjamin's voice cut through the red haze, and Tom realized he was shaking Buck like a rag doll. He released his hold on him and stepped back, appalled by his own lack of control.

"Get him out of here," Tom said. "Lock him up until I decide what to do with him."

As Benjamin lead the protesting Buck away, Tom sank back into the chair. He could hold Buck twenty-one hours without charging him.

That gave him twenty-one hours to try to find out if Buck was a cold-blooded killer who had not only murdered India but had also attacked Peyton, or if he was just a dumb putz who just happened to run into the wrong woman at a bar.

The day seemed endless to Peyton. She played with Lilly, cleaned the kitchen and then paced the floor, wondering if her life would ever be normal again.

What if Tom never found the person who had attacked her? What if he never found out why India had kidnapped Lilly and who had killed India?

How could Peyton hope to live a normal life if there was no resolution to the crimes? She would forever be looking over her shoulder, wondering if her attacker might strike again, this time with deadly results.

If she wasn't thinking about the crimes, then her thoughts were filled with Tom. She wanted to believe that there was some sort of future with him, but she knew she was probably fooling herself.

At three o'clock when her doorbell rang and she peeked out and saw Rachel, she was thrilled by the distraction of a visit from this new friend.

"I just thought I'd stop by and check in on you," Rachel said as Peyton led her into the kitchen.

"I can't tell you how happy I am to see you. Sheriff Grayson doesn't want me leaving the house, and even though I don't need to go out for anything, I'm suddenly feeling like a prisoner in my own home." Peyton gestured her to a seat at the table. "Can I get you something cold to drink? Iced tea or a soda?"

"Tea would be great. How are you feeling?"

"A little rough today," Peyton admitted. "It's not too bad if I don't breathe too deeply or move too fast. And God forbid I sneeze or cough."

"And there's still no clue as to who did this to you?" Rachel asked.

"No. None." Peyton placed the tea on the table, then took the seat across from Rachel. "Where's your daughter?"

"Ah, twice a week I take her to Portia's Playpen for play time. She has a wonderful time and mommy gets a little downtime to visit friends or just sit and read a book without interruption."

"I've arranged for Portia to take care of Lilly when I start teaching. I have to confess, since the kidnapping the idea of leaving her with anyone is a little frightening."

"Portia is amazing, and she'll love your Lilly just like you do," Rachel replied. "Trust me, you're putting her in good hands."

"That's good to know. Tom only had good things to say about Portia. He said she and Caleb dated while they were in high school."

"Everyone just assumed they'd get married and live happily ever after, but I guess not all high school romances can go the distance."

"I didn't have time to have a high school romance," Peyton said. "I was working two jobs in high school and living on my own."

For the next hour the two women visited, sharing pieces of their past, talking about their present and their hope for the future for their daughters.

It was just after four when Rachel stood to go home. "I need to get dinner started. David likes to eat at five-thirty on the dot, and I'm trying a new chicken recipe tonight."

Peyton walked with her friend to the door. "I really appreciate you stopping by," she said as she unarmed the security system. "I'm eager to make lots of friends here in Black Rock."

Rachel offered her a friendly smile. "Consider Dawn and me two of your first."

Peyton was still smiling after Rachel left. Once Tom solved the issue of who had attacked her and life returned to normal, she knew she was going to like it here in Black Rock.

It was going to be a wonderful place for Lilly to grow up. There was nothing nicer than a real small town, with a café where everyone gathered and people who looked out for each other.

By eight that evening she'd put Lilly down for the night and had broken down and taken one of her pain pills. Feeling a bit woozy, she settled on the sofa and turned on the television, comforted by the sound of a sitcom.

Tom had called just after five to check in on her, and she'd assured him she was fine and didn't need anything. He'd told her there was nothing new on the cases, and the call had been brief.

As she stretched out on the sofa she felt as if her mind had fuzzy edges, thanks to the pill she'd taken. "You should just go to bed," she said aloud. Maybe she'd feel better in the morning.

Deciding to call it a night before she got too groggy, she got up from the sofa and turned off the television. She was headed down the hallway when the doorbell rang.

Instantly her heart leapt in her chest. Maybe it was Tom. She hurried to the front door and peeked out, surprised to see Rick.

"Rick, what a surprise," she said as she opened the door to allow him in.

"Sorry it's so late, but court has been cancelled for tomorrow so I thought I'd drive out to see you and Lilly."

He smiled apologetically. "I know I should have called, but it was a spur-of-the-moment decision, and I was afraid you'd tell me to wait until tomorrow. And to be honest, I was worried about you."

How she wished she could love him. Everything would be so less complicated if she and Rick were in love. But she wasn't in love with him. She was in love with Tom.

"Lilly's already down for the night," she said. "And as you can see, I'm fine, although a little dopey because I took a pain pill."

He stepped into the foyer and closed the door behind him. "I couldn't believe it when I heard what happened to you." The warmth of his eyes faded. "I couldn't believe I didn't break all your ribs when I kicked you."

Peyton stared at him, for a moment wondering if the medication was tampering with her ability to understand. "What?"

"Ah, Peyton, you've been a real pain in my ass. If India had done what she was supposed to, I wouldn't have to be here now to finish the job."

Peyton took a step back from him and tried to make sense of what he was saying. "You knew India?" The question whispered out of her on a labored breath.

"I met India at a bar one night after work. She was hanging around looking for a date, and by the end of the night she was crazy about me. She loved me enough to do anything for me. She moved here to get close to you and gain your trust."

He frowned with irritation. "But when it came right

down to it, she couldn't do it. She couldn't kill Lilly and she couldn't kill you. But you know what I always say, if you want a job done right, you should do it yourself."

He pulled a length of rope from his pocket, and horror washed over Peyton as she tried to make sense of what was happening.

Chapter 12

It was nearly seven when Sam brought Tom a pile of papers he'd copied off the Internet. "That's everything I could find about Rick Powell. He must like being in the news. I don't think he misses a photo or interview opportunity."

"Thanks, Sam. And now you'd better get out of here. Loretta is going to have my head for keeping you so late."

Sam grinned. "You know Loretta's bark is worse than her bite. Good night, boss," he said as he walked out.

Tom shuffled the papers together and stuck them into a manila envelope. He'd go over them at home. He left his office to see Caleb and Don Walker, another young deputy, ready to work the night shift.

"Heading out?" Caleb asked.

Tom nodded. "Going home."

"I see you're taking work home with you," Caleb said and pointed to the manila folder.

"Yeah, I'm checking into Rick Powell. Aside from Buck and Cliff, he's the only person in Peyton's life. And speaking of Buck, go ahead and cut him loose. We've got no evidence to hold him, and I'm doubtful that anything will suddenly show up. He might as well sleep in his own bed tonight."

Don stood and grabbed the jail keys from the top drawer of the desk. "For a tough guy, he's been doing a lot of whining since he got locked up."

Tom smiled. "You know the old saying—the bigger they are, the harder they fall. I'm out of here."

As he walked out into the hot night air he thought of Peyton. What was she doing right now? Was she curled up in bed reading a book? Was she parked in front of the sofa watching television? Was she missing him?

The last thought made him slam his car door harder than necessary. It didn't matter whether she missed his presence in her house or not. He didn't belong there.

By the time he got home, a weariness had invaded his soul. There was no question that he hadn't slept well on Peyton's sofa. He'd been haunted by memories of making love to her, angered by the vision of the angry bruises that darkened her skin and frustrated by the fact that he hadn't already made an arrest.

His house seemed big and empty as he walked through the door. The silence was deafening. He realized he'd grown accustomed to Peyton's voice filling the quiet, to Lilly's sweet coos adding music.

Once again irritated by his own thoughts, he walked into the kitchen, put on a pot of coffee to brew and sat at the table and spread out the items Sam had printed off the Internet.

Before he started looking at anything he poured himself a cup of coffee and called Brittany's cell phone. As usual, it went directly to voice mail.

He sipped his coffee and for a moment allowed himself to think about his missing sister. Even though he didn't want to believe anything sinister had happened, his frame of mind was dark, and he couldn't help but admit that he was worried about her; the worry was growing bigger and bigger with each hour that passed without contact from her.

He told himself not to worry, that there was absolutely no evidence to show that his sister might be in any trouble. Besides, he had real crimes in front of him to solve, and until he knew something different about Brittany, that's where he needed to focus.

He began to sort through the information Sam had pulled up on Rick Powell. Sam wasn't kidding: it seemed that Rick enjoyed having his mug in front of the cameras.

There were social events, charity appearances and work-related stories. The first thing Tom did was separate it all into three piles. Once he had the items separated he started on the work-related items.

It didn't take long for Tom to realize Peyton was

right—the man was definitely ambitious. Tough on crime, and with a winning smile, he was a perfect candidate for a future in politics, and there were several interviews where he told the reporter that's where he intended to eventually land.

In one interview given just after the date of Lilly's birth, he was asked about his single status, and Rick hadn't mentioned a word about Peyton or the baby.

In fact, the interesting thing for Tom, as he perused through the social and charity piles, was that although many of the photos had been taken during the time when Peyton and Rick were a couple, she was in none of them. He was either photographed alone or with whoever was in charge of the function he was attending.

Why wouldn't he take Peyton with him? Why hadn't he mentioned Peyton to his friends or family? The birth of a baby was something to celebrate. Perhaps Rick had never accepted Lilly's presence.

Tom frowned and shoved the paperwork aside, then poured himself a fresh cup of coffee and leaned back in his chair.

His mind whirled with the information he had about India, about Tom and Buck. He felt as if he was missing an important link.

Why had India taken Lilly? It didn't ring true that she'd simply taken the baby to give to a second cousin in the next town, a woman who was capable of having her own children. Tom had decided not to arrest the young couple. He believed their story, that they thought what they were participating in was a legal adoption of an unwanted baby. They had fully cooperated with him, and he believed their only crime was being young and uneducated.

He sipped his coffee and stared out the window, working the pieces of the puzzle around and around in his head in an attempt to make sense of everything that had happened.

Rick Powell was an assistant district attorney. India Richards had a record of petty crimes. Was it possible their paths had crossed at one time or another in Wichita?

It was definitely possible.

So why would Rick want to get rid of Lilly? Because he didn't want to be a dad? Peyton had said he was upset when he'd found out she was pregnant but that he'd eventually come around.

She had insisted that she'd told Rick he didn't have to be a part of Lilly's life, that he didn't have to pay child support or do anything that he didn't want to do.

It still didn't make sense, but he didn't trust Rick Powell. He wasn't convinced that the man was innocent in all of this. Maybe he had these feelings because there was no viable suspect left. Cliff Gunther had been cleared, and Tom's instinct told him Buck was nothing but a loser whose only crime had been trying to hook up with a new young woman in town.

It suddenly seemed important that he tell Peyton his concerns about Rick. Although Rick hadn't been around much since the kidnapping and Tom knew that Peyton refused to consider that he might have anything to do with what had happened, Tom would feel better erring on the side of caution.

As he grabbed his cell phone from his pocket he wondered if he was just manufacturing a reason to call her, to hear her voice before he went to bed.

He opened his phone and got ready to dial, then clicked it shut once again. He'd talk to her in the morning, when his head was clear and exhaustion didn't weigh so heavy on his shoulders.

He got up from the table and shut off the coffeemaker then headed for his bedroom. Maybe everything would be clearer in the morning after a good night's sleep.

"What are you doing?" Peyton asked as Rick grabbed her by the arm and lead her into the kitchen. He forced her into a chair and began to tie her there.

"I'm sorry to say that you and Lilly are going to be the victims of a terrible home invasion." He tied her tightly into the chair. "But before I take care of you and Lilly, I need to set the stage—a broken window, some items taken out." He flashed her a confident smile. "Believe me, I've prosecuted enough of these cases to know how to set a scene."

"I don't understand," Peyton said, her heart beating so fast she feared she might pass out. "Why, Rick? Why are you doing this?" She couldn't believe this was the man she'd dated, the man who had stood next to her as she'd delivered their daughter.

His smile faded, and for the first time since she'd known him anger blazed in his eyes. "I have dreams,

Peyton. Big dreams, and you and that kid are in my way. I never signed on to be a father. You were just a girl I was dating for a while. Did you really think it could be anything more than that? You come from nothing. Your mother died in prison. Your mere existence in my life is a detriment to where I want to go, to who I want to be."

She stared at him, wondering how she'd missed the selfishness, the utter depravity he possessed. "You don't have to be part of our lives," she said frantically. "I told you I'd never expect anything from you where Lilly was concerned."

"That's what you say now, but you would have changed your mind. You would have sucked the life out of me for the rest of Lilly's life."

"That's not true, Rick. Please, you have to believe that I want nothing from you. You can live whatever life you want, go after your dreams and we won't bother you." Tears blurred her vision as the reality of the situation penetrated through her foggy head.

Danger hadn't intruded into her home; instead she'd invited it in. She should have been wary when she saw him on the porch at this time of night, but she hadn't been thinking clearly.

"Rick, if you leave now I promise I won't say anything about this. You'll never hear from me again." She was begging not for her own life, but for Lilly's life. "At least leave Lilly alone." She struggled against the rope that held her hands to the chair rungs behind her, but there was no give.

"You don't get it." Wild rage rode in his eyes as he looked at her. "I'm going places, and in the world of politics an illegitimate child and the daughter of a convict are trouble. But a man who lost his daughter and his girlfriend to a violent crime is a figure of compassion. You're worth far more to me dead than alive."

He backed away from her. "Now I've got to take care of some things. If you scream, I'll kill Lilly right in front of you."

As he went into the living room, tears raced from Peyton's eyes. She pulled on the ropes, trying to free herself from the chair, but it was no use.

She heard the sound of the front door open and then close, and when there was no resulting alarm sounding she realized she hadn't reset the alarm after she'd let him inside.

A moment later she heard the tinkle of a window breaking in one of the rooms. Setting the scene. The police would assume that the killer had come in through the broken window. She guessed that he'd take her television and stereo, he'd steal what little jewelry she had and whatever else that would make it look as if she'd been the victim of a robbery gone bad.

A clawing panic rose up in the back of her throat. Once he was finished setting the scene he would kill her, then he'd kill Lilly.

She had to do something. She had to save her daughter, but how?

She heard him re-enter the house, and every muscle in her body tensed. She wished she'd moved a million miles from Rick. She wished she had the strength to break the rope and get free to fight for Lilly's life. Finally she wished she would have followed her heart and told Tom that she loved him.

The ring of the phone cut through the air as Rick came back into the kitchen. He picked up the cordless and looked at the caller ID screen with a frown. "It's Tom."

"If I don't answer he'll think something is wrong," she said.

"Get rid of him, and if you do anything stupid, Lilly will be dead before he can get here, and I promise you I'll make her suffer." He clicked the phone on and held it to her ear.

"Tom," she said. The scent of Rick's cologne, the feel of his body heat so close to her, made her want to vomit.

"Hi, Peyton. I just thought I'd give you a quick call to see how you're doing."

"I was just on my way to bed. I'm exhausted and my ribs are sore. I took three of the pain pills the doctor gave me about a half an hour ago, so I really don't feel like talking."

"Oh, then I guess I won't keep you. I'll come by in the morning—there are some things I want to discuss with you."

Peyton willed herself not to sob, not to scream. "Okay, I'll see you in the morning," she replied. As Rick disconnected, the sob she'd been fighting against erupted out of her.

She swallowed hard and looked up at Rick. "You murdered India, didn't you?"

He leaned with his slim hip against the counter. "She was a loose end. Talk about a stupid woman. She actually thought I was going to marry her, that we were going to live happily ever after."

"She was waiting for you at the motel. That's why she didn't run away after she took Lilly." She wanted to keep him talking. As long as he was talking, Lilly remained safe.

"I told her I'd come and get her, take her back to Wichita with me. She was in love with me. All I had to do was tell her that you and Lilly were ruining my life. Unfortunately, when it came to killing you and Lilly, she didn't have the guts to follow through."

Crazy love, Peyton thought. That's what India had felt for Rick. It had been the sick kind of obsession that really had nothing at all to do with real love.

"This all would have been over if that old man hadn't come running to your rescue in the park," Rick continued. "You'd be dead, Lilly would be gone and that would have been the end of things."

"You're going to be caught," Peyton said. "You're never going to get away with this. You're going to be the first person Tom looks at when I'm gone."

"Ah, Peyton, do you really think I'd come out here to take care of you without having a solid alibi lined up for myself? India wasn't the only woman in my life who would do anything for me. Right now there's a woman in Wichita who will swear under oath that I was at her house this evening having dinner. I'm five steps ahead of Sheriff Tom Grayson. Now, it's time for me to finish up my work here."

As he once again left the kitchen, an overwhelming sense of despair swept through Peyton. She had hoped that Tom would get the message and sense something in her voice, realize that she wouldn't take that many pain pills while home alone and with Lilly in her care.

Lilly! Her heart cried in anguish. Her sweet baby. Was he in there with her now? Placing a pillow over her face? Wrapping his fingers around her neck?

As the minutes ticked by and death crept closer, for the first time in her life Peyton felt all hope seep away.

Chapter 13

He'd had no intention of calling her, but as Tom had undressed for bed, he couldn't resist hearing the sound of her voice before going to sleep.

As he got into bed, the brief phone call played in his head. She'd sounded fine, so why did an electric current of worry zing through him?

She'd told him she'd taken three pain pills, but he'd had to fight with her to take two. She'd said she'd taken them a half an hour before he'd called, but when he'd given her the two pills, within a half an hour she'd been nearly comatose.

Something wasn't right. Had she been trying to tell him that something was wrong, that she was in trouble? He leapt out of bed as if the sheets were on fire.

It took him only seconds to get dressed again. As he left the bedroom he used his cell phone to call Caleb.

"Caleb, it's me. Meet me at Peyton's place."

"What's up?" Caleb asked.

"I think she's in trouble. Don't pull up in the driveway. Park down the street and we'll go in quietly. Wait for me. I should be there in five minutes."

Tom clicked off as he raced to the kitchen and grabbed his car keys. His heart thrummed an anxious rhythm as he left the house and got into his car.

He hoped he was wrong. He prayed the sick feeling in his gut was all a mistake. He'd get to Peyton's and she would be fine.

Maybe he'd misunderstood what she'd said about the pills. Maybe he was making a big deal out of nothing. He hoped so.

Still, with each minute that passed the anxiety inside him grew more intense. His heart beat so rapidly he heard it banging in his ears.

Buck Harmon had been released from the jail. Had he gone to Peyton's house? Or was it possible somebody else was there, somebody who had so far flown under the radar?

It took only minutes to reach Peyton's street. He parked his car next to the curb half a block away and a moment later Caleb pulled up behind him.

"What do you think is going on?" Caleb asked as the two men met at the front of Tom's car. "There's no vehicle in her driveway. Everything looks peaceful."

"I called her a few minutes ago and she said

something that didn't sound right. I don't know, maybe I'm overreacting, but I have a bad feeling and thought I should come over here and check things out."

"How do you want to handle this?" Caleb asked.

Tom frowned as he looked up the street at her house. "Let's head to the back and see if we can look through the windows and see if anything looks off. I don't want to go to the front door, because if somebody is in there with her, we don't know what the response might be. With Peyton and Lilly inside, I don't want to take that kind of a chance."

Caleb nodded. "Then let's do it."

Together the two moved through the dark of the night like silent shadows. They cut through the neighboring yards to reach Peyton's place. Tom mentally cursed as he saw the six-foot privacy fence. He'd forgotten all about it.

Caleb cupped his hands and gestured that he'd boost Tom over the fence. Tom nodded and with his brother's help dropped to the grass on the other side.

The back of the house was before him. Lights burned in both the kitchen and the living room. Tom drew his gun and approached the kitchen window, which was the easiest one to see inside.

He raised up to peek in and his heart crashed into his ribs, momentarily stealing his breath away. Peyton was tied to a chair. Her chin was on her chest and her eyes were closed.

Was he too late? Grief crashed through him—grief coupled with an anger he'd never known. He had to get to her. He left the window and moved to the back door. It was locked, but he used the butt of his gun and broke the glass so he could reach through and unlock it.

As he entered the kitchen, Peyton's head snapped up and her eyes widened, but instead of relief, they held fear. "It's Rick," she whispered. "Save Lilly. If it's not too late, please save my baby."

Tom felt gutted as he left her in the kitchen and slid into the living room, his gun leading the way. He had no idea if Rick had heard his entry into the kitchen, had no idea if the man was waiting for him now with a weapon of his own.

Every muscle in his body was tensed as he saw that the television and stereo were by the front door, obviously ready to be carried outside and taken away.

So he was going to make it look like a robbery gone bad. Tom's blood boiled, but beneath the rage was a fear so intense it cramped his stomach. If Rick had done anything to that precious little girl, then Tom wouldn't try to arrest him, he'd kill him.

He crept silently down the hallway, trying to get a handle on which room Rick was in, but he heard nothing that would give him any indication.

He whirled into the first doorway he came to, the bathroom, but it was empty. The next room was the spare bedroom, and once again there was nobody inside.

Lilly's room was next, and as Tom stepped inside he saw Rick leaning over the crib. "Freeze!" Tom said, fighting his impulse to pull the trigger.

Instantly Rick straightened. He whirled around and

threw something at Tom. For a moment Tom thought he'd thrown Lilly, and he dropped the gun in an effort to catch the baby, only to discover it was a stuffed bear.

Before he had time to process it, Rick was on him. They fell to the floor, where both of them grappled for the gun that had slid beneath the rocking chair.

The gun slid farther away, and Tom managed to drag Rick toward the doorway. Rick swung a fist and connected with Tom's jaw. His head snapped back and he tasted blood, but it fed the rage and he landed a hard right on Rick's nose.

More fists flew and they both gasped for air as the fight continued. The gun was forgotten as they exchanged blows.

Finally it was another fist to Rick's nose that brought the fight to an end. Rick fell to the floor on his back, his breathing labored and his eyes closed as Tom got to his feet.

He reached beneath the rocking chair to retrieve his gun, then looked into the crib and gasped a sigh of relief as Lilly's bright blue eyes met his and she smiled.

He looked up to see his brother standing in the doorway. "How long you been there?" he asked.

"Long enough," Caleb replied.

"Thanks for the help," he said dryly. Gently he picked Lilly up from the crib and suddenly remembered the bruises on Peyton's body. When he passed Rick's prone body, he kicked him hard in the ribs. Rick moaned and curled up in a fetal ball.

"Get this piece of crap locked up," he said. "I need to take care of Peyton."

As he left the room, Caleb was handcuffing Rick. Tom hurried down the hall toward the kitchen where he could hear Peyton sobbing.

As he entered the room and she saw Lilly in his arms she began to laugh and cry at the same time. Tom placed Lilly in the bouncy chair on the table, strapped her in, then moved to Peyton.

He began to work the ropes in order to free her. "Thank God you came," she exclaimed. "He was going to kill us. He killed India and he attacked me that night in the park."

"You were smart, Peyton. Telling me that you took three pain pills sent all kinds of alarms through my head," he replied.

"I wasn't smart," she scoffed, obviously stifling new sobs. "I let him in. I just opened the door and invited him inside."

Tom managed to get the last rope off her and she stood and turned to face him. Before he knew it she was against his chest, burrowed into him as her body trembled with residual emotion.

Tom tried to keep himself rigid, uninvolved, but as she wrapped her arms around his neck he gave into his need to hold her, to assure himself that she was really all right.

She cried against his chest as he held her. "It's over, Peyton," he said softly. "It's finally over, and he can't hurt you again."

When he finally released her, she went to Lilly and pulled the baby into her arms. "I need to get a full statement from you," he said. "And I'm going to have to get a couple of the boys in to process this scene." He pulled his cell phone from his pocket. "Why don't you go sit on the sofa and we'll get this all done as soon as possible."

He mentally shifted from man to sheriff. There were things that needed to be done to assure a successful prosecution of Rick Powell.

It was after ten by the time his team began to photograph and collect evidence. Tom had taken a detailed statement from Peyton as she held a sleeping Lilly.

"This is going to take a while," he said to her. "You want to go to a motel for the night?"

She shook her head. "I'm fine here. I don't think I could sleep anyway. I keep replaying it all in my head. I can't believe Rick would go to the lengths he did for some grand future he had planned for himself. And India, she was under his spell."

"At least she wasn't so crazy to follow through and kill you and Lilly," Tom replied. The relief he felt that it was all over was intense. She was safe, and hopefully nobody would ever try to hurt her again.

It took most of the night to completely process the house and Rick's car, which they had found parked down the street. It was five o'clock in the morning when the team packed up and Tom and Peyton were once again alone in the house. Lilly had been put back in her crib when Tom eased down next to Peyton on the sofa.

"You finally have your life back," he said to her.

"Rick is smart and he knows the system," she said with a touch of apprehension.

He took her hand in his, wanted to whisk away the last of her fear. "He's gone for good, Peyton. It doesn't matter how smart he is or how well he knows the system. He's going to spend the rest of his life behind bars. Now, what you need more than anything is to get some sleep."

He started to pull his hand back, but she squeezed and refused to let it go. "When I was tied to that chair all I could think about was Lilly and you." Her gaze held his, and in the depths of her beautiful blue eyes he saw a wealth of emotion.

"All I could think about was that I'd never get a chance to see Lilly walk, and she'd never get a chance to play with little friends or go to school." Tears sparkled in her eyes. "And the other thing I kept thinking about was the fact that I hadn't told you that I was falling in love with you."

Her words hit him from out of left field, and for just a moment an incredible joy filled him, but it was followed quickly by some of the deepest regret he'd ever felt.

He pulled his hand from hers and got up from the sofa. "Peyton, don't."

"Don't what?" She got up and stepped toward him. "Don't fall in love with you? It's too late, Tom. I can't stop what I feel in my heart, and I'm sure if you look deep in your heart you'll have to admit that you care for me more than a little bit."

"Of course I care for you," he replied uneasily. He didn't want to have this conversation. The light shining from her eyes as she looked at him shot into his heart. He knew he was going to hurt her and he hated it, hated himself for doing it.

"Peyton, you told me you want to be a priority in somebody's life, that you were tired of being a distant third. In my life that's all you'd ever be. I've already had my priorities with my ex-wife and my daughter."

"But, Tom, they're gone. They've been gone for a long time. Isn't it time for you to open your heart to love again? Won't you give yourself a chance at happiness?"

Tom felt himself closing in, closing off. There was a part of him that wanted to embrace what she offered, but there was a bigger part of him that wanted to run as fast and as far away as possible.

"Find a nice man, Peyton. Our town is full of them. Find a man who will love you and Lilly to distraction, a man who has an open heart and a loving soul."

"I've already found him." Tears escaped her eyes to shine on her cheeks. "What happened to India Richards was a tragedy. What almost happened to me and Lilly would have been a tragedy, but the real tragedy in all of this would be if you don't allow yourself to find happiness again." Her voice trembled. "I want you to be happy, Tom. I want you to love again, and if you can't find that with me, then I hope you'll find that with another woman." She stepped back from him. "I just wanted you to know how I feel about you. It suddenly seemed important that I tell you."

"Peyton, this has been a crazy time. I'm sure once things settle down and get back to normal you'll realize your feelings for me aren't as strong as you think they are," he replied. His chest felt tight, filled with an emotion he couldn't identify and didn't want to look at too closely.

She looked at him sadly. "Tom, I know the difference between crazy love and the real thing, and I know what's in my heart." She released a weary sigh. "Go on, you need some sleep and so do I. I guess I'll just see you around."

"I'll be in touch as the case goes forward," he said. There were a million things he wished he could say to her, but the words were trapped someplace deep inside him, in a place he refused to access.

There was nothing more to say, nothing left to do but leave. He turned and walked toward the front door without a backward glance.

As he stepped outside, dawn was just beginning to light the eastern sky, but even the promise of a new day couldn't lighten the weight of his heart.

He'd never meant to hurt her. He'd been clear with her from the very beginning that he didn't want a wife, any children in his life. He shouldn't feel responsible for her feelings, and yet he did.

Sleep, that's what he needed more than anything. He needed to put Peyton's words of love out of his head.

Eventually she'd meet somebody who would be the perfect man for her and a wonderful father for Lilly.

You're in a box of your own making. Jacob's words jumped into his head. *You never gave yourself time to grieve.*

Tom had intended to go right home, but he found himself at the entrance of the cemetery where Kelly was buried. He parked the car and stood just outside the iron gate, emotion like a steel band pressing hard into his chest. He hadn't been here since the funeral.

His head filled with echoes of a little girl's laughter, her sweet voice shouting "Daddy" whenever he came home from work.

Before he realized what he was doing, his feet carried him through the quiet dawn across the lush grass to her final resting place.

The headstone was tiny and held simply the name of Kelly Marie Grayson. Tom stared at the headstone and realized his brother had been right.

Jacob had been right. He hadn't taken the time to grieve for his daughter. He'd had a wife who had been overwhelmed with her grief, her guilt, and he'd had to keep it together for her.

But now there was nothing between him and his grief, and as it ripped through him he sank down to his knees in the dewy grass next to her grave. For the first time in five years, Tom wept for the child he had lost.

It took two full days for Peyton to really embrace the fact that the danger was over and her life was truly her own. The bruises on her ribs were beginning to heal, and she suffered no nightmares from her trauma—nothing except for the heartache that held the name of Tom.

She'd hoped that after he'd had a good night's sleep he would have a magical epiphany and realize he loved her, but as the first day passed and then the second, she accepted the fact that he hadn't felt the same way that she'd felt about him.

What surprised her more than anything was that once the story broke of what had happened to her, the town of Black Rock seemed to gather to offer her support and friendship.

Women stopped by with casseroles and little toys for Lilly. Even Walt Tolliver came by with a charm made of aluminum foil that he insisted would keep the aliens at bay.

It was the evening of the third day after Rick's attack on her that Peyton loaded the stroller into the trunk of her car. Lilly was already in her car seat in the back of the car, and the early evening air was warm, but not uncomfortably so.

As Peyton slid in behind the steering wheel she fought a little flutter of anxiety. She was meeting Rachel and Dawn and their children at the park.

When they'd called earlier in the day to invite her along, her first impulse had been to turn them down. She wasn't sure she was ready to face the place where she'd been nearly kicked to death.

But then she realized she didn't want to be afraid to

go back there. She hoped that the park would be a place of many happy memories for her as Lilly grew up.

As she pulled up to the park the two women were waiting for her. As she shut off her engine she wished it were Tom meeting her here for a walk in the park after dinner.

"Foolish woman," she muttered to herself as she got out of the car. She had to put Tom out of her head, somehow get him out of her heart.

She gave Dawn and Rachel a bright smile as she pulled Lilly from her car seat, then went to the back of the car to retrieve the stroller.

"Here, I'll get it," Dawn offered and took her car keys from her.

Within minutes the three women were on a park bench with Lilly in the stroller and Dawn and Rachel's kids on the playground with a handful of other children.

"Another week and a half and school will start. Are you all ready?" Dawn asked.

Peyton nodded. "I've been working on lesson plans and can't wait to get started." Part of her eagerness to get to work was that she hoped with the hours of the day filled she would finally be able to stop thinking about how safe she'd felt in Tom's arms, how safe and right it had been when they'd made love.

A pleasant, light breeze accompanied their conversation, and Peyton felt a sense of satisfaction as she realized these women were new friends…good friends.

Aside from the fact that seeing Tom on the streets of the small town, running into him in the café or at town functions would hurt, she knew she was on her way to building a wonderful life here for herself and her daughter.

She didn't know how long they'd been sitting and visiting when Tom's sheriff's car drove slowly by.

"Evening patrol," Rachel said.

"I've always felt safe here in Black Rock," Dawn said. "I think that's why what happened to you was so shocking to everyone."

"It must be a consolation for everyone in town that Rick wasn't from here and had no real ties to the community except for the fact that I happened to move here," Peyton said.

Dawn nodded. "You never want to believe that a friend or neighbor could be responsible for that kind of violence." She gave Peyton a bright smile. "At least it's over."

"Thank goodness," Peyton exclaimed.

Tom's car appeared again, and this time he turned into the park entrance. Instantly Peyton's muscles all tightened. She wasn't ready to see him. Her emotions were still too raw.

She narrowed her eyes and watched as he parked the car and got out. He looked achingly handsome in his khaki uniform, and her heart squeezed in her chest as he approached.

"Evening, ladies," he said.

They all returned his greeting.

Tom looked at Peyton. "Could I speak with you for a moment?"

"Of course," she said. He probably needed to talk to her about the case against Rick. As a victim of a crime and with him being sheriff, she knew there would have to be a certain amount of interaction between them. She got up from the bench.

"You can leave Lilly here," Rachel offered. "We'll keep an eye on her while you two talk."

Peyton hesitated a minute, then reminded herself that these women were truly her friends and she could trust them. Tom led her away from the benches to stand beneath a nearby tree. Peyton steeled her heart against the onslaught of emotion he evoked in her.

"How are you feeling?" he asked.

"Better every day," she replied.

"Rick was transported to Wichita right after his arrest. He's been officially charged with murder and attempted murder. It's a solid case, so you don't have anything more to worry about."

She forced a smile to her lips. "I wasn't worried. I know you did your job well, and there's no way he's walking on a technicality. But thanks for the information." She turned to go back to the women, but he grabbed her arm with his hand.

"Peyton, wait."

She turned back to look at him. She just wanted this conversation over. The smell of his cologne made her remember being held in his arms.

"When I left your house the other morning, I remembered something my brother Jacob had said to me. I had spoken to him about you after the night we'd made love. I told him what an amazing woman you were, that I found myself having strong feelings for you, but that I had no intention of following through on anything. He told me that I was in a box of my own making, that I'd never really grieved for all that I'd lost, and I told him he was crazy. But that morning after leaving you, I found myself at Kelly's grave and I realized he was right—I hadn't given myself a chance to grieve."

"Oh, Tom, I'm so sorry." She couldn't help the fact that her heart ached for him.

"No, don't be. That morning at Kelly's grave I realized that I couldn't move forward until I'd let go of the past. My grief for her filled my heart so completely I didn't have room for you or for Lilly."

He leaned with his back against the tree, his eyes distant as he stared across the expanse of the park. "I didn't know I had that many tears in me, but that morning they all came out." A faint pink tinged his cheeks, as if he was embarrassed by this admission. "I cried like a baby, and for the past two days I've been numb."

She couldn't stand it anymore. She had to touch him. She wanted to console him, to somehow help him heal. She took one of his hands in hers. "There's no shame in crying for somebody you love."

"I know," he agreed. "The thing is, I woke up this morning and the grief was gone, the numbness had passed and all I was left with were my feelings for you."

Peyton felt as if her heart stopped beating, as if

everything around her faded away and there was only Tom. "What feelings?" she asked softly.

"I'm falling in love with you, Peyton. I don't know if I can be the man you and Lilly want, the man you need in your life. All I know is that I want to try."

Her heart exploded with happiness as he took her into his arms and his lips met hers. The kiss was like nothing they'd shared so far. Yes, it had the wild passion, the gentleness of the other kisses they had shared, but this one simmered with sweet promise.

As the kiss finally ended, he smiled down at her. "You know by morning we'll be the talk of the town."

She laughed. "I'm already the talk of the town for all the wrong reasons. I don't mind being the talk of the town if it means I'm with you."

He dropped his arms from around her. "We've been through a life-and-death situation, we've shared our pasts and we've made love. Maybe it's time we go out on an actual date."

"Just name the place and the time," she replied.

"How about right now. We'll have some dessert and coffee at the café."

With a wicked little grin, she placed her palm against his cheek. "How about we have coffee at the café and dessert at my place."

His eyes flared with a heat that warmed her from her head to her toe. "We'll make it a quick cup of coffee," he replied, his voice thick and smoky deep.

As Peyton and Tom walked back to Lilly's stroller, Dawn and Rachel smiled at them with a knowing gaze.

"Looks like you're settling in here just fine, Peyton," Dawn said.

Peyton smiled as Tom took control of Lilly's stroller. "I think I'm at the beginning of a wonderful life," she said. "I'll see you guys later, Tom and I are headed to the café."

"You go, girl," Rachel said.

As Peyton walked with Tom and Lilly toward the cars, she remembered the dreams that had sustained her through her terrible childhood.

Despite the odds, she'd managed to get her education, land a wonderful teaching job and move to a quaint little town filled with good people. Best of all, she'd found a man to love, a man who found his capacity to love again after suffering a tremendous loss.

It was a new beginning for both of them, and as Tom gently lifted Lilly from her stroller and kissed her sweet little cheek, Peyton felt her future calling. She knew that future was going to be filled with warmth and laughter and the love of an amazing man.

Epilogue

He stood in the building that had become his playroom. Hidden by a grove of trees and brush in the center of a pasture, and after some major renovations, the old barn was perfect.

The wooden horse stall enclosures had been torn out and replaced by steel bars, creating individual jail-like enclosures, each with its own plumbing.

It was a perfect place for him to keep his collection, a place where nobody would bother him and, most important of all, isolated and insulated to assure that nobody could hear the screams. Ah, the screams. There was nothing more exciting than the sound of a woman screaming in fear, in pain.

He walked to the first "cell" and gripped the cool iron bars in his hands. She lay inside on a cot, her hair a spill of dark silk against the white pillowcase.

Brittany Grayson. She was beautiful and bright and all his. At the moment she was still drugged, as she had been for the past two weeks. Today he'd stop giving her the drug that had kept her out of it since the moment he'd taken her.

Eventually she'd regain consciousness and realize she was a prisoner, his prisoner. He wanted to be here when that moment happened. He wanted to see the fear etched deep into her pretty eyes, see it stretch her mouth into a scream.

He pulled up a nearby chair and sat, prepared to wait for that moment to occur. As he waited his gaze shifted to the other cells. There were five of them, and eventually they would all be filled. Then the games would truly begin. He fought a shiver of excitement at the thought.

Maybe a blonde next time, he thought. Or perhaps a redhead. After all, variety was the spice of life. He had to admit he was vaguely surprised that Brittany had been missing two weeks and nobody had raised an alarm.

Soon the alarms would sound. Soon the entire town of Black Rock would be in an uproar as they realized pretty young women were disappearing.

In the meantime, he was savoring the first of his collection. He couldn't wait for Brittany Grayson to wake up.

* * * * *

April 2010 marks the release of the fourth book in Harlequin Intrigue's exhilarating new, dare-you-to-put-it-down MAXIMUM MEN *series.* ENIGMA *by Carla Cassidy! Read on for an exciting sneak preview!*

The hospital room was dimly lit and silent except for the faint voices coming from the television mounted on the wall opposite the bed.

Willa Tyler had insisted that the television be on day and night in the room despite the fact that the man in the bed had been in a coma for the past six months. She liked to believe that somewhere in the sleeping recesses of his mind he might hear the sound of laughter from a sitcom and want to join the fun.

Even though it was late and she was officially off duty, she always made his room her last stop before heading home.

She moved silently into the room and for a moment just stood and looked at him. He was something of a miracle patient. He'd been found on the side of the road, more dead than alive after having been hit by a drunk driver.

Nobody had expected him to live through that first night, but he'd hung on, and over the past six months all his physical injuries had healed. But his mind remained asleep, and Willa was beginning to wonder if he'd ever wake up again.

Harlequin offers a romance for every mood!
See below for a sneak peek
from our paranormal romance line,
Silhouette® Nocturne™.
Enjoy a preview of REUNION by USA TODAY
bestselling author Lindsay McKenna.

Aella closed her eyes and sensed a distinct shift, like movement from the world around her to the unseen world.

She opened her eyes. And had a slight shock at the man standing ten feet away. He wasn't just any man. Her heart leaped and pounded. He reminded her of a fierce warrior from an ancient civilization. Incan? She wasn't sure but she felt his deep power and masculinity.

I'm Aella. Are you the guardian of this sacred site? she asked, hoping her telepathy was strong.

Fox's entire body soared with joy. Fox struggled to put his personal pleasure aside.

Greetings, Aella. I'm the assistant guardian to this sacred area. You may call me Fox. How can I be of service to you, Aella? he asked.

I'm searching for a green sphere. A legend says that the Emperor Pachacuti had seven emerald spheres created for the Emerald Key necklace. He had seven of his priestesses and priests travel the world to hide these spheres from evil forces. It is said that when all seven spheres are found, restrung and worn, that Light will return to the Earth. The fourth sphere is here, at your sacred site. Are you aware of it? Aella held her breath. She loved looking at him, especially his sensual mouth. The desire to kiss him came out of nowhere.

Fox was stunned by the request. *I know of the Emerald Key necklace because I served the emperor at the time it was created. However, I did not realize that one of the spheres is here.*

Aella felt sad. Why? Every time she looked at Fox, her heart felt as if it would tear out of her chest. *May I stay in touch with you as I work with this site?* she asked.

Of course. Fox wanted nothing more than to be here with her. To absorb her ephemeral beauty and hear her speak once more.

Aella's spirit lifted. What *was* this strange connection between them? Her curiosity was strong, but she had more pressing matters. In the next few days, Aella knew her life would change forever. How, she had no idea….

*Look for REUNION
by* USA TODAY *bestselling author
Lindsay McKenna,
available April 2010, only from
Silhouette® Nocturne™.*

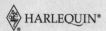

HARLEQUIN
Ambassadors

Want to share your passion for reading Harlequin® Books?

Become a Harlequin Ambassador!

Harlequin Ambassadors are a group of passionate and well-connected readers who are willing to share their joy of reading Harlequin® books with family and friends.

You'll be sent all the tools you need to spark great conversation, including free books!

All we ask is that you share the romance with your friends and family!

You'll also be invited to have a say in new book ideas and exchange opinions with women just like you!

To see if you qualify* to be a Harlequin Ambassador, please visit
www.HarlequinAmbassadors.com.

*Please note that not everyone who applies to be a Harlequin Ambassador will qualify. For more information please visit www.HarlequinAmbassadors.com.

Thank you for your participation.

BAP09BPA

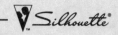

SPECIAL EDITION

**INTRODUCING A BRAND-NEW MINISERIES
FROM *USA TODAY* BESTSELLING AUTHOR**

KASEY MICHAELS

SECOND-CHANCE BRIDAL

At twenty-eight, widowed single mother
Elizabeth Carstairs thinks she's left love behind
forever....until she meets Will Hollingsbrook.
Her sons' new baseball coach is the handsomest
man she's ever seen—and the more time they
spend together, the more undeniable the
connection between them. But can Elizabeth
leave the past behind and open her heart to
a second chance at love?

FIND OUT IN

SUDDENLY A BRIDE

*Available in April
wherever books are sold.*

HARLEQUIN® Romance®

ROMANCE, RIVALRY AND A FAMILY REUNITED

THE BRIDES
of
BELLA ROSA

William Valentine and his beloved wife, Lucia, live
a beautiful life together, but when his former love Rosa
and the secret family they had together resurface,
an instant rivalry is formed. Can these families
get through the past and come together as one?

Step into the world of Bella Rosa
beginning this April with

Beauty and the Reclusive Prince
by
RAYE MORGAN

Eight volumes to collect and treasure!

HER MEDITERRANEAN PLAYBOY

Sexy and dangerous—he wants you in his bed!

The sky is blue, the azure sea is crashing
against the golden sand and the sun is hot.

The conditions are perfect for
a scorching Mediterranean seduction
from two irresistible untamed playboys!

Indulge your senses with these two delicious stories

A MISTRESS AT THE ITALIAN'S COMMAND
by Melanie Milburne

ITALIAN BOSS, HOUSEKEEPER MISTRESS
by Kate Hewitt

Available April 2010 from Harlequin Presents!

www.eHarlequin.com

HP12910